Fairy Tales Unleashed

NAIMA SIMONE

DEDICATION

To Gary. 143.

NAIMA SIMONE

ACKNOWLEDGMENTS

To God, from whom all of my blessings flow. Not only could I not have done this whole journey without You, I don't want to. Thank You for Your love, faithfulness and increase.

To Gary. I love you more than words can say. Your support and encouragement humbles me. Thank you for being the hand at my back pushing me during the times I wanted to stop. Love you.

To Debra Glass. Thank you for this GORGEOUS cover and for helping me put the books of my heart back out there. Your help, guidance, enthusiasm and friendship are priceless. Truly priceless. And so are you.

To AJ Nuest. Thank you for the wonderful editing job you did on this book. Even years later, it's still smooth, clean and beautiful. You gave me my first lesson in what it looks like for an editor and author to have a wonderful relationship. And now a friendship. Thank you!

NAIMA SIMONE

BARGAIN WITH THE BEAST

Desperate to keep her neighborhood community center open, Gwendolyn Sinclair seeks out Xavier St. James, her childhood friend…and brother of her dead fiancé. Xavier possesses the funds necessary to keep the center open, but he offers another bargain—a devil's bargain: submit her body to his pleasure for seven days and the building doesn't close its doors.

Left scarred from an accident, Xavier is bitter, resentful and alone. When Gwendolyn reappears in his life, need and loneliness overrides conscience and he proposes an arrangement she can't afford to refuse. With the woman he has always wanted—but could never have—finally in his bed, he hungers for more. Her heart. But could she come to love a beast?

Author Note

The "Beauty and the Beast" quotes found at the beginning of each chapter are from eighteenth-century French novelist Jeanne-Marie Leprince de Beaumont, as well as eighteenth-century fairy tale collectors, the Brothers Grimm. Beauty consented to dropping all extortion and blackmail charges as part of the prenuptial agreement.

CHAPTER ONE

"What will you have, Beauty?" said her father.

"Since you have the goodness to think of me," answered she, "be so kind to bring me a rose, for as none grows hereabouts, they are a kind of rarity."—Beauty and the Beast

"Show me someone who says they don't want anything from you and I'll show you some real estate in the land of Wake the Fuck Up."—Xavier St. James

"When did the freak show come to town?"

Gwendolyn Sinclair stiffened, caught off guard. The comment—heavy with derision and horror—had come from her left. Attempting to be unobtrusive, she glanced over her shoulder and spotted a tall young man whose curled lip had transformed his features from handsome to disdainful and arrogant.

"What are you talking about?" the petite blonde next to him asked.

He dipped his chin to indicate someone across the room. Gwendolyn followed the couple's gaze.

Her heart stopped. Then resumed with a dull thud that echoed in her ears. Goose bumps pebbled her arms and a thin film of sweat dampened her palms and underarms.

Xavier St. James.

Business mogul, former playboy and society-column darling. The man who'd been avoiding her phone calls and e-mails for weeks. The man she'd attended this pretentious gathering of Boston's social elite to corner.

"You'd think he'd at least cover that thing with his hair or even makeup, for God's sake. Why should we have to look at it?"

As the meaning of the young man's words struck her, Gwendolyn gasped as if she were the target of his derision. Hurt and anger mushroomed in her chest. She clenched her teeth to force back the torrid spew of words burning her tongue. She inhaled a deep breath, held it and counted to ten...then twenty. Getting thrown out of the event would only succeed in making a scene and harm her chance at attaining her goal. She smiled grimly. Though it might be worth the risk to yank the stick out of the guy's ass.

"Stevie Wonder could spot that mutation. Mr. Perfect." A horrible, malicious glee entered his companion's taunt. "To think he once could have had any woman he wanted. Now he probably has to pay for it." The woman snickered and her delight in someone else's pain and misfortune sickened Gwendolyn. *Bitch.*

"People like him have it all and believe they're better than everyone else only to find out they're just like the rest of us. Human and touchable."

The remainder of the couple's conversation faded as Gwendolyn pivoted on the heel of her stiletto and walked off. Her stomach couldn't handle their spite *and* the dry chicken cordon bleu served at dinner.

She wended through the bejeweled and tuxedo-clad crowd, skimming past an aged socialite who would probably regret imbibing too many glasses of champagne in the morning and the young man who was the recipient of her amorous, drunken overtures. God. She silently snorted. Though the people around her belonged to another tax bracket, eliminate the designer clothes and you-paid-*what*-for-that jewelry and they were just the same as those she lived among in her Dorchester neighborhood—ready and eager to take advantage of free food, drink and gossip.

She drew to a halt several feet from the tall, forbidding man she'd once called a good friend. He stood alone like a child exiled to the time-out corner on the playground. Gwendolyn tilted her head to the side, studying him. For him to *not* be surrounded by a throng of people was as new as the inch-thick scar bisecting the left side of his face from hairline to hard chin.

At thirty-four, Xavier had lived a charmed life—until a year ago. As admittedly elitist and exclusive as Boston's privileged society circle could be, the exotic St. James family had been accepted and revered. And Xavier, the elder of two sons, had been the golden child of his family and its international real estate empire. An excellent student and athlete in high school and college, he'd excelled in the family business and rocketed to the office of vice president of operations. As hard as he'd worked, he'd played with the same single-minded focus. Socialites, models, actresses. Xavier had romanced legions of women and graced the glossy pages of many magazines and social columns. And when he fell in love and became engaged, his fiancée had been a gorgeous elegant woman—his equal in wealth and social status. Success. Affluence. Love. Yes, he'd held the world in the palm of his hand...

Gwendolyn fisted her fingers, fighting the urge to cup his damaged cheek, battling the need to curl against his chest and drown in the rhythm of his heartbeat under her ear. But the stranger who surveyed the ballroom and the partygoers with a cold stare didn't invite warmth or even human touch.

Cautiously, she edged around a laughing couple and stole closer. From her vantage point, it appeared as if the terrible accident responsible for stealing both his father and physical perfection had never occurred.

The honeyed skin and thick golden-brown hair bound at his nape bespoke a heritage of hot sands and sensual pleasures, while the tall frame, wide shoulders and narrow hips called to mind the lush green hills and magic of his father's lands. Persian and Irish—Xavier was an exotic blend of the two countries' finest traits.

Then she glimpsed the marred left side of his face. The scar didn't inspire the disgust she spied on the patrician features of the guests or the perverse glee from the spiteful couple. Nor did pity well inside her chest. The scar didn't ruin his features. On the contrary. The long ridge of raised flesh only enhanced his beauty, magnified the unblemished perfection.

"Gerald. Melanie." His dark baritone slid over her skin like the finest silk. A shiver raced down her spine and poured through her veins in a molten stream. A voice like his should've been locked up in Pandora's box along with Hope to keep the world safe—or at least her libido.

"Xavier." An older couple jolted to a halt in front of him, flustered. The silver- haired gentleman extended his hand, voice full of strained joviality. His wife, Melanie, wore a similar bright smile—a bit too dazzling to be genuine. "How are you? It's been awhile." Immediately a deep scarlet surged up Gerald's neck and bloomed in his cheeks.

"Yes, it has," Xavier agreed, accepting Gerald's hand and briskly pumping it up and down before releasing it. "It would've been the museum gala a year ago…right before the accident and Dad's death."

Damn. Gwendolyn winced.

More color flooded Gerald's face. He ducked his head and cleared his throat while his wife lifted fluttering fingers to her throat. Sympathy pricked Gwendolyn at the couple's obvious unease. How the hell could they respond to such a blunt statement that smacked of accusation?

But Xavier stared at them, full lips unsmiling, the lines of his face hard, cold. He didn't appear moved or apologetic over the discomfort he caused. Surprise sang through her. The man she'd known wouldn't have deliberately embarrassed another person. Xavier's natural charm had been one of the reasons people gravitated toward him.

He remained silent as the older gentleman cleared his throat and jerked on the bottom of his jacket to straighten nonexistent wrinkles. His wife studied the silver shoes peeping out from under her gray dress, the diamond bracelet on her thin wrist— anywhere but Xavier's face.

"Well," Gerald cleared his throat again, "yes. I believe that was the last time. I still say it was a shame about your father and…and…"

Xavier arched an eyebrow.

"Gerald, the Carlyles are waving us over." Melanie tugged her husband's arm. She beamed another brittle smile and, with a murmured apology, hustled her husband away. The older man turned, but not before Gwendolyn glimpsed the relief swamping his expression.

Irritated at the couple and Xavier, she moved forward, eliminating the scant space separating them. "You did that on purpose."

His back stiffened slightly. The perfectly cut black tuxedo jacket did a poor job of concealing the power and strength of his body. The urge to stroke her fingers across the hard muscle raged so strong, she clenched her fingers until the short nails bit into her palms. As if in slow motion, Xavier turned and, for the first time in three years, she came face-to-face with her former childhood friend.

And the man she'd been in love with even while engaged to another—his younger brother. His dead younger brother.

Joshua. She swallowed hard, but nothing could force the acidic burn of remorse and shame scalding her throat to disappear. Guilt had dogged her for years like a relentless stalker. Joshua St. James had offered her friendship, stability and love. What she wouldn't give to have loved him the way he'd needed—the way he'd deserved from a fiancée.

Ruthlessly, she slammed the door on those debilitating thoughts. She couldn't afford any distractions while facing this intimidating stranger with the familiar face.

If Xavier was surprised to see her, his green unblinking gaze did not reveal his astonishment.

"I did what on purpose?" he asked, his bland tone nearing the point of boredom.

Hell, she nearly reached out to check his pulse.

No *Hi, Gwendolyn, long time, no see.* Or *Gwendolyn, how the hell are you?* Nothing but the same hard, blank mask. It alarmed and annoyed her.

"Hijacked them. Put them on the spot." She ticked the options off on her fingers. "Take your pick."

Xavier's lip curled and the faint smile contained a wealth of derision. "I'm just keeping them honest. Instead of giving me sidelong glances and whispering about my face behind my back, I'm offering them a full frontal view."

That view packed the power of a sledgehammer. True, he was no longer flawless, but this didn't make him any less beautiful. Instead of a golden Adonis, he'd become Odysseus—mortal, battle-worn and scarred, but victorious because he'd made it through a tragedy that would have broken most people.

Wow, she grimaced inwardly. Flowery much? Greek gods, battles… She needed to pop *Clash of the Titans* out of the DVD player.

She caressed his features with her gaze. God, she'd bargain her soul and only pair of Christian Louboutins to stroke the hard jut of his cheekbone or trace the arrogant slope of his thin, patrician nose.

Brush the firm, sensual bow of his upper lip and the full cushion of the lower curve. That erotic dream of a mouth would be soft—as certainly as any overture at gentleness would be rejected.

She inhaled and mentally stepped back from the precarious ledge she hovered on. "You're punishing them." *And yourself.*

If possible, his expression hardened further, the harsh lines drawn so tight his flaming-jeweled stare blazed. *Oh damn.* She played the words back in her head. And winced.

"W-wait…" she stuttered. "Hold on. I didn't—"

"Am I punishing you, Gwendolyn?" he murmured, eyes narrowing. "Is looking at me such a hardship?"

She opened her mouth to object, but snapped her lips shut. One glance at the grim line of his lips and the dangerous glint in his eyes and she swallowed her explanation. Why bother? Xavier wouldn't believe her concern was for *him*, not the shallow socialites he'd once called friends. Yes, he punished them for their hypocrisy by refusing to be regulated to a shameful secret everyone whispered about. And yet, by confronting their thinly disguised disgust and horror, he inflicted wound after wound to his heart—a heart Xavier would probably deny possessing.

Gwendolyn waved a hand. "That's ridiculous."

"Is it?" he drawled, cocking an eyebrow.

She sighed. "Xavier—"

"What are you doing here, Gwendolyn?"

Irritation flared at his abruptness. But since she'd come to the event seeking him, she tamped it down and plastered a serene smile on her face.

"I was invited," she replied. "I used to attend this gala with Joshua. I guess they never removed my name from the invitations list."

If the mention of his brother affected him, Xavier hid it well. "So you're attending in memoriam of my brother?"

Gwendolyn bit back a blistering response at the droll question. *The community center. Remain focused on the community center.*

"Not exactly." She bared her teeth in a tight smile. "I came here to see you."

* * * * *

Xavier studied the five-foot-nine-inch beauty before him.

Gwendolyn probably believed she hid her annoyance well. Yet

even as a kid, she'd worn her emotions on her lovely face.

Lovely… No, the word paled when describing the delicate bone structure, almond- shaped eyes and wide, mobile mouth. Striking. Powerful. Stunning.

Sexy as fuck.

Her toffee-colored hair, only a few shades lighter than her smooth skin, had been drawn back into a classic bun. Still, he recalled the explosion of unruly spirals that proclaimed her biracial heritage as if he'd seen her just yesterday instead of three years ago. Tonight the tamed mass accentuated her arresting features, emphasized the chocolate-brown eyes, the high cheekbones. He clenched his jaw. The only sight capable of competing with her face was the visual orgasm of her body.

Xavier lowered his inspection and swallowed a hungry groan. Hell, those curves and dips could make RuPaul straight. Or envious. Her full breasts would fit his wide palms perfectly. The small indentation of her waist and feminine flare of her hips would provide the perfect spot to grip while he fucked her long and hard. For kicks and giggles, throw in long, slim legs that would wrap around his waist, her heels bouncing against his ass as he plunged and withdrew from what he dreamed would be a tight pussy.

Shit.

His breath quickened. His heart stuttered. If he didn't leash his imagination, he would scandalize the good citizens of Boston by tenting his tuxedo pants with a huge hard-on.

But then, his dead brother's woman had always possessed the power to make him desire something unavailable to him…something beyond his reach.

Her.

For the first time in seven months—since the day his ex-fiancée had cheated and left him for another man—he experienced an emotion besides antipathy and bitterness toward a beautiful woman. Unlike others of the fairer sex, Gwendolyn didn't avoid his face as if one glance would transform her to stone. She didn't stammer well-bred phony excuses to extricate herself from his company.

No. As she'd stated, Gwendolyn had come to see him. That simple sentence shouldn't have had the effect of a fist squeezing his cock.

"Well, you found me, Gwendolyn," he murmured with a small

quirk of his lips. The puckered skin bisecting the left side of his face pulled tight with the gesture and the reminder of the disfiguring scar destroyed any warmth her declaration had ignited. "It must be important for you to brave the beast."

She scowled. "It's not the scar that makes you a beast. It's your attitude."

Anger simmered in his chest and he narrowed his gaze. "Watch your tongue, Gwendolyn."

"Or what?"

"Or you may just find it caught." *By my mouth, then on my cock.*

As soon as the words whispered across his mind, he envisioned her leaning over him, her full, sensual lips pressed to his, their tongues engaged in an erotic duel. Pictured those same lips forging a damp path down his chest and abdomen to his throbbing dick. *Jesus.* He fisted his fingers as if to capture the imagined silken glide of her hair over his wrist and hand. As if even now the hot, tight clasp of her mouth tightened around his shaft and sucked him close to the beautiful edge of oblivion.

If she could perceive the desire and need shredding his gut into ribbons, she'd shut the fuck up and run.

"I didn't come over here for this," Gwendolyn grumbled. She lifted a hand, but stopped just short of thrusting her fingers through her hair. Lowering her arm, she aimed another black scowl at him as if it were his fault she couldn't grab the bright strands. "I need to talk to you."

"That's what we're doing."

"In private."

He surveyed the crowded ballroom in a long, exaggerated sweep before settling back on her. "Now is not a good time."

Damn, he enjoyed needling her. She had always stirred that reaction in him. Even when she'd been engaged to his brother Josh, she'd been the little sister he'd kidded and affectionately teased.

Well, maybe "little sister" was a bit of an embellishment... After all, wondering what your sibling looked like naked was not only illegal, but sick.

And for years, he'd wondered.

"It will have to be a good time, Xavier. You've put me off for months now and I only have two weeks left."

Her accusation jolted him from thoughts of soft, smooth skin, tangled limbs and writhing bodies. "What the hell are you talking about?"

She sighed. "I've called your office at least a dozen times in the last few months. I've dropped by only to wait for hours while you were on a 'conference call'." She air- quoted with her fingers, a sure sign her annoyance had ratcheted to royally pissed off. "Did it ever occur to you I might not have been dropping by to shoot the breeze but because I needed you?"

Needed him? *Him? Shit.* She'd located and pressed his Easy button.

"Fine," he growled and hated himself for being interested...for being susceptible to this woman. Gripping her upper arm and ignoring how her bare skin branded the flesh of his palm, he towed her in the direction of the small study off the ballroom. She stumbled behind him but righted herself and kept up with his quick stride. Remorse assailed him and the attack of guilt served as a reminder why he had to get rid of Gwendolyn Sinclair.

Over the past year, he'd struggled with his father's death, his fiancée's—*ex*- fiancée's, damn it—betrayal, ostracism by his peers and a disfigurement that sent kids screaming for their mothers. At some point in the tragic clusterfuck, he'd grown numb. His heart had atrophied to a withered lump in his chest where nothing or no one could hurt him.

Now Gwendolyn had shown up and gifted him with glimpses of a happier past and ghosts of emotions he'd become accustomed to existing without.

Yeah, he would listen to her for old time's sake, as well as Josh's. But after that, she had to go.

And never come back.

CHAPTER TWO

"My name is not 'My Lord'," replied the monster, "but Beast…do not imagine I am to be moved by any of your flattering speeches. But you say you have got daughters. I will forgive you, on condition that one of them come willingly and suffer for you."—Beauty and the Beast

"Blackmail is such an ugly word. Effective…but still very ugly."—Xavier St. James

"You have five minutes. Starting now."

Xavier shoved his hands in his pants pockets and the motion drew his jacket away from his chest. Damn, it was wide. Gwendolyn dragged her gaze over his flat stomach, slim hips and down to… *Whew, boy.* She glanced away from the impressive bulge even the most artful cut couldn't hide.

Jesus, what was wrong with her? One glance at his crotch and she was hot with anticipation.

"Time's a-wasting." The taunt jerked her attention to his face. *Focus, dammit. Focus.* His hooded scrutiny and the grim line of his mouth were inscrutable. Oh sweet baby Jesus, did he know where her eyes had been trained? Or worse, what thoughts had flirted through her mind? She groaned silently. God wouldn't be so cruel. At least she prayed He wouldn't be…

"I've been trying to get in touch with you—" "Been over that."

"To ask for your help," she gritted and bulldozed ahead despite his rude interruption. "The community center is in need of a grant."

"The community center? A grant?" His eyebrows slammed into a dark vee and incredulity smothered his voice. "You need me because of money?" He tipped his head back on his shoulders and emitted a sharp bark of laughter she would have been an idiot to label humorous. "Isn't that just fucking perfect?"

"I don't need your money...or rather your family's foundation money," she corrected. "The community center does. If we don't receive funding, we'll have to close our doors."

"Same difference." He tilted his head forward and his emerald stare studied her as if she were splayed on a glass petri dish under a microscope. "The foundation has a committee to determine who receives the money. It's not my decision. Go through the application process like everyone else."

"It *is* your decision. You have your finger on everything that bears the St. James name." She stole closer. "It's the community center, Xavier. Where you, Josh and I met. You learned how to play basketball there. It's just as important to the neighborhood now as it was then. If not for the center, so many kids would be in gangs instead of on teams. Or receiving a destructive education on the streets instead of the tutoring needed to help them graduate high school. We need that grant, Xavier."

Her voice wavered with the passion burning in her chest. But the huge, old building settled smack in the middle of Roxbury *was* her passion. As chief administrator and program director, Gwendolyn spent much of her time at the center. Just like she'd passed most of her afternoons and evenings there as a child—her single-parent mother too preoccupied with chasing the youth she'd accused her daughter of robbing.

Renee Sinclair had resented the child she'd birthed at seventeen years old. By the time Gwendolyn turned eight, Renee valued nightclubs and various boyfriends over her daughter. In her mother's list of priorities, Gwendolyn ranked beneath sex, men and alcohol, but above church—and only because Renee was usually too hung over to attend a Sunday service. Survival had taught Gwendolyn to cook simple meals of omelets and hamburgers, clean their cramped, lonely apartment and get herself to and from school.

She'd met the St. James brothers at the center one hot June afternoon—twelve-year- old Xavier and ten-year-old Joshua. Their father had been heading up a construction project nearby and instead of having his sons hang around the demolition site every day, he'd sent them to the neighborhood community center. One summer had turned into years. She had become best friends with Joshua, and Xavier—as the older brother—had looked out for both of them.

Though from different backgrounds, the three of them had established a tight bond. And when Xavier, and then later she and Joshua, had gone off to college, their friendship had endured. If not for the community center, she would've never had the St. James brothers in her life.

Maybe she alone cherished those memories of happier days. She scanned the harsh, severe lines of Xavier's face, the flat, shuttered eyes. She might as well have been asking a mountain to feel, to empathize. Come to think of it, a rock probably contained more emotion.

"So you want to bypass the application process and have me influence the foundation's decision on your behalf." He twisted his lips into a merciless caricature of a smile. "Based on what? Basketball memories and you fucking my brother?"

The cruel words punched a hole in her chest. Pain and humiliation radiated from the jagged wound. Of course the accident and the events following the crash—his father's death, his fiancée's abandonment, the rejection of his "friends"—had affected him. But the man staring down at her with cold, pitiless eyes didn't resemble the Xavier St. James she'd known…and the difference had nothing to do with his scar. Warm humor, kindness and compassion had been integral aspects of his personality, but those traits had disappeared, leaving this aloof, cynical stranger who wore her childhood friend's face.

Gwendolyn sucked in a shallow breath. Fine. In her mind, she snatched off her earrings, dragged her hair into a ponytail and donned her sneakers—the classic "sista" move symbolizing she was ready to box.

"Far be it from me to impose on sentiment you don't possess," she cooed in a tone her mother would have termed nice-nasty. "But when I'm the only one playing fair in a process where the door is closed to me before I even knock then yes, I have no problem with circumventing that same process." She bared her teeth in a feral smile. "And instead of memories, how about I base my request on discrimination and prejudice? Or disenfranchisement? Do those words work better for you?"

"Two minutes."

The cool reminder of the elapsing time detonated her temper like a lit match tossed onto a batch of napalm.

"It must be nice to dwell in an ivory tower where you can lord over the world but not be a part of it. Pretend the dirty masses don't exist except to keep your empire running." The anger poured from her lips in a furious torrent of uncensored words and resentment. She should care, should put a halt to the furious tirade. Yet the diatribe, now started, could not be contained.

"But the people who enable you to live like a prince are the same ones in need of your foundation's help. Not the Beacon Hill Beautification Society. Or the local country club women's polo team. Real people with real issues, like finding resources that will provide a way out of poverty-stricken and crime-ridden neighborhoods. Like equipping children with a sufficient education when their schools have a shortage of textbooks and supplies."

Gwendolyn stalked forward until mere inches separated them. Heat radiated from under his white silk shirt, but it was like banked embers under the gleam of his intent gaze. Under normal circumstances, she would have proceeded with caution. But these weren't normal circumstances.

"What are you talking about?" he asked quietly.

An ominous shiver skated down her spine. For a heavy moment, silence descended over the room like the lull in a storm right before it struck with full force.

"Have you bothered to check and see where your community service funds have been allocated?" Her anger hadn't dimmed, but she regarded him like prey keeping a wary eye on a stalking predator. "Your family's foundation was established to serve the needs of the greater Boston community. That community stretches past Charles Street, Xavier. For the past four years, your foundation's committee has awarded grants to two country clubs, a beautification society and an Ivy League polo team. I don't know about the other applicants who don't hail from such wealthy, gentrified origins, but I was given the runaround for weeks about the status of my application before being informed I was mistaken. I had not applied."

She closed her eyes at the helpless fury consuming her even a week later. Throw in Xavier's refusal to intervene in the slanted, shady practices of his family's charity and she wanted to rail at him, cause him physical harm to siphon off some of the frustration and bitterness welling inside her.

"Gwendolyn."

She opened her eyes and met his gaze again. The rigid lines of his face remained stoic.

"What?"

"I'll look into it. And if what you say is true, I promise you the review and decision process will change at the foundation."

She believed him. Xavier might be a cold bastard now, but he'd always been a man of his word and she didn't think something so elemental could have been altered by the accident.

However, his assurance did little to alleviate her predicament. "Thank you. I'm sure your query will certainly help someone next year. As for today, it doesn't change anything. If the community center doesn't receive aid, it will close in two weeks."

He regarded her for long, silent moments. Gwendolyn endured the disquieting inspection though she longed to avert her gaze to the floor, the ceiling, the damn wallpaper—anything except his distant, gorgeous face.

"What are you willing to do to save the center, Gwendolyn?"

Surprise snatched the air and words from her throat. An image swam before her—a cat with emerald eyes batting its paw at a mouse, toying with the unlucky rodent that bore an uncanny resemblance to her.

Leery and more than a little suspicious, she studied him. "I-I don't know what you mean."

"Exactly what I said. What are you willing to do—to sacrifice—to save the community center?"

The better question would be what *hadn't* she sacrificed to save the center? She'd agreed to a cut in salary, had extended her hours to compensate for the teachers' shorter shifts. She opened the building at seven a.m. and locked the doors well after seven p.m. When she dragged into her small Dorchester apartment each night, her feet ached, her stomach grumbled and her head usually throbbed with worries about parents, bills and funding.

But right on the heels of those sacrifices came the rewards. The laughter of the children as they played kickball. The pride straightening the shoulders of the older teens as they walked across the stage to accept their high school diplomas. The gratefulness in a parent's eyes as they picked up their child after work, knowing their son or daughter had been safe instead of in trouble on the streets.

"Anything," she vowed. Yes, she was long on hours and short on pay, but the rewards couldn't be numbered...or lost. "I'll do whatever it takes to keep it open."

A calculating gleam entered Xavier's eyes and she almost retracted the pledge.

Oh God. So that's what the devil looks like when he buys a soul.

"I can't interfere with the process at this late date," he said, drawing his hands from his pockets and crossing his arms. "Whether the committee's actions were right or wrong, to step in now would penalize the recipient and, regardless of how the decision came to be, that's not fair."

Tough shit. She snorted and Xavier arched an eyebrow.

"There's another alternative." He paused and she resisted the urge to glance over her shoulder and measure the distance to the door. Once again she was the mouse to his cat. Except he'd surpassed the toying stage and was licking his paws in preparation for dinner—*her*. "I'll personally fund the community center for a year. I'll donate a check in the exact amount of the grant."

Joy soared in her chest even as relief flooded her veins, washing away the stink of desperation she'd worn for months. She hadn't expected him to—

Suspicion delivered a ringing reality slap. Wait a minute. She narrowed her eyes. The offer was generous yet the man she'd encountered this evening didn't strike her as the magnanimous kind. Niggling doubt warned her a booby trap loomed one step after her agreement to his gift.

"That's generous of you," she hedged. Then paused. "What's the catch?"

"You," he murmured. "You spend seven days and nights with me...in my bed." His lashes lowered and he stared at her from under a hooded gaze that promised sex and sin. The timbre of his voice had deepened, conjuring images of dark, hot nights and naughty acts she'd read about, dreamed about...touched herself to. "In other words, Gwendolyn, give me your body for the next week and your precious community center remains open."

* * * * *

Even as he spoke—as his lips shaped the words—part of him couldn't believe he'd vocalized the ultimatum. God, how far had he sunk? This was Gwendolyn, for fuck's sake! He'd watched her grow from a knobby-kneed eight-year-old into a woman. Yet as her shock faded and fury tighten her face into a contemptuous mask, lust rose up beside the shame, capsizing the guilt until only need remained.

She was a bright, living flame—searing, passionate…damn, so much passion. She gave everything, held nothing back. Could he survive being on the receiving end of such fierce heat? Shit, he wanted to find out. He *hungered* to find out.

Since Evelyn left him, his sexual encounters had been reduced to escorts, well- compensated to pretend they found him irresistible. But he could only con himself into believing he didn't notice their flinches of revulsion or pity for so long. Fucking his fist had become more preferable…and less humiliating.

Gwendolyn didn't ignore his disfigurement or avoid direct eye contact. No. Instead she squared off with him, challenging him. And it was hot as fuck. He skimmed down her smooth shoulders, slender arms and clenched fingers. Her wine-colored dress draped in clean folds down her full breasts, narrow waist and hips. His cock throbbed in greedy anticipation and he resisted the urge to fist his erection and squeeze to alleviate some of the ache.

More than his next breath, he wanted to lift the long sweep of material hiding her long legs, pretty thighs and sweetly curved ass. His palms itched as he conjured the silky glide of her smooth skin and the wet, creamy flesh of her pussy.

Wet for him.

Yeah, he may be a grade-A bastard for blackmailing her into fucking him, but damn if he could rummage up a conscience about it. His dick overruled principle.

"That's not funny," she bit out. "And your joke is in poor taste."

"I don't joke about half a million dollars." He paused. "Or fucking."

"What happened to you, Xavier?" The outrage bled from her tightened features, leaving behind the pity he detested. "Did that witch you called a fiancée hurt you so deeply you would sink to," she waved a hand back and forth between them, "to this?"

He stiffened. Like hell they would discuss Evelyn. He didn't want to think about her. Didn't want to remember walking into their bedroom to discover his soon-to-be- bride—the woman he'd loved—riding another man. Didn't want to recall her tear-filled eyes as she blamed his disfigured face for her betrayal.

"Are you involved with someone?"

"What?" Her brow crinkled as if she were puzzled at the brusque question and switch in subjects.

"Are you involved with someone?" he repeated.

Her head jerked as if an invisible fist had clipped her chin.

Impatience jabbed at him, hardening his voice. He couldn't contain the urgency stemming from the alarm constricting his chest as he waited for her answer. If she responded in the positive, he would call the deal off. The knowledge he could lose her with one word clawed at him. But the pain and humiliation of Evelyn's betrayal continued to haunt him like a stubborn ghost refusing to go into the damn light. No matter how much he wanted—needed—Gwendolyn, he wouldn't inflict that torment on another person.

He was a bastard, an asshole and pathetic enough to extort sex from a woman he wanted, but he would *never* force her to betray a man she loved. So much for his dick overriding principle. It appeared he had one moral standard left.

How fucking inconvenient.

"No," she snapped. "Do you think I would even consider your...your blackmail if I were seeing someone?" Anger curled her lip. Yet beneath the ire a note of pain quivered, adding a slight tremble to her objection.

He steeled his heart against an annoying prick of sympathy.

"The time for consideration has passed. Yes or no, Gwendolyn," he demanded, the ice freezing his veins mirrored in his tone. "Make a decision. It's your choice."

"What choice?" she spat and crossed her arms, turned her head away. A muscle ticked along the delicate, vulnerable line of her jaw and he almost rescinded the gauntlet he'd cast down. Almost.

"Simple, sweetheart." He eliminated the inches separating them and shifted forward, bringing them chest to chest, thigh to thigh. He lifted his hand and, pinching her chin in a firm but gentle grip, forced her to face him. Her small, sharp gasp brushed the skin on his throat and savage triumph surged through him. This close she couldn't hide the rapid rise and fall of her chest or the small whimper she bit off.

His heart pounded in his chest like an animal attempting to free itself from its prison. Gwendolyn wanted him. She may not like her attraction for him or even be ready to admit it, but the body couldn't lie. If a slim chance of rescinding the ultimatum had existed, the shudder of her breath across his skin obliterated that possibility to hell.

"Either give me your body for seven days or relinquish your precious community center in fourteen. Sacrifice yourself to the beast or watch the doors of the center close. Is it going to be you or the kids you claim to love so—"

"You're right." She wrenched her chin from his grasp, but didn't shy away from his close scrutiny. "You are a monster." The insult stabbed him in a heart he'd believed no longer existed. "And I accept your...terms," she whispered.

The victory possessed an acrid tang even as his pulse pounded and his gut knotted with anticipation. In days he would be balls-deep inside this stunning woman. Nothing, not even the tiny flash of remorse, could conquer the need to find oblivion in her pussy. Would she be fierce, demanding her pleasure? Or would she reveal a shier side, one he would enjoy shocking with the acts he planned to exact from her? Would her sheath cream for him, easing the tight fit around his cock—

"Don't misunderstand, Xavier. I'll lie on my back for you because the other choice sucks worse. But when the week is over, know you'll have taken more than my body. You'll have stolen my memories of the man you were."

She pivoted and stalked toward the door. The rigid spine and the sultry sway of her hips in the deep-red dress waved at him like a red flag to a raging bull. Shame and lust mingled, swirling together in a toxic mixture. He rushed across the room. His chest slammed her back and only the anchor of his arm snaked around her waist prevented her from tumbling to the floor.

He didn't pause to analyze or reassess his actions. His cock, nestled in the crease of her ass, commandeered all rational thought. The bottom curve of her breasts pillowed over his arm, the mounds a warm, sensual weight. But her full, sexy ass...the soft cushion cradling his dick... He groaned, ground his erection into her flesh and groaned again.

Lust claimed him. He tightened his hold around her waist and gripped her hip with his free hand, restraining her for the slow, hard strokes of his cock. The miniscule section of his brain not yet consumed by arousal comprehended Gwendolyn didn't fight him. She arched in his arms, her spine forming a perfect bow. The sweet curves of her bottom circled against his dick in an eye-crossing grind. Hell no. The low whimpers weren't pleas for escape—they were encouragement. Sweet need.

"One taste, baby," he muttered and released her hip to cup her chin and angle her head back. He dragged his lips along the exposed, graceful line of her neck. Fresh and pure, the taste of her skin was like water to a thirsty man. He savored another sip. The muscles in her throat bobbed under his teeth as he grazed a path to the slope of her shoulder.

"So good," he praised. "So damn good." He transferred both hands to her waist and whirled her around. As her chest bumped his, he swallowed her soft, surprised gasp into his mouth. The flavor of her... *Jesus*. Like the honeyed *bamieh* his mother used to make when he was a boy combined with the punch of whiskey-laced coffee his father enjoyed after dinner. Sweet. Potent. Addictive. He plunged between her parted lips, tongue-fucking her mouth the same way he hungered to thrust his cock into her body.

She gripped his arms and clung to him as if he were her anchor in the midst of a violent tempest. He sucked on her tongue, not allowing her to withdraw. Not allowing her to leave him. The need clawing his gut transformed him into the ravenous beast he called himself.

He clenched the material of her dress and bunched it in huge fistfuls, drawing the skirt up her thighs. The muted swish of silk sweeping over skin caressed his senses, waltzed over his nerve endings in a sexy duet of anticipation and need.

She dug her nails into his arms and the bite stoked the fire in his balls. But when he tucked his hand between their bodies and dipped between her thighs, the flame raged into an inferno.

Damn, she was soaking wet. Awe filled him, momentarily eclipsing the gnawing hunger. *For me. She's wet for me.* He groaned. Flexed his fingertips against her swollen flesh.

"No!" Gwendolyn cried. She wrenched free and stumbled backward a couple of steps before steadying herself. For several long moments, only her labored pants and his harsh breathing reverberated in the room. The tension thrummed like a living, breathing entity. Head lowered, hands fisted alongside her thighs, she stood as still as a statue, warm flesh transformed to cold stone.

Look at me! Look at me, dammit! The demand screamed like a wild gale in his head, but fear squeezed his throat. Shame glued his lips shut. Would he identify disgust in her dark gaze? Disgust and disbelief because she'd allowed him—a disfigured beast— to touch her? Or worse, abhorrence because she'd been aroused, her hoarse whispers begging for more of his touch, her tongue tangling with his, her sex soaked with cream?

Coward.

He snarled, loathing scalding him as if he'd been dipped in an acid bath. He didn't have the nerve to examine her features and find the answers.

"No, what?" he drawled. "Don't make you wet? I believe that ship has sailed, sweetheart."

* * * * *

Gwendolyn sucked in a deep breath and held it in vain hope of extinguishing the hurt like fingers snuffing out a candle's flame. The pain ricocheted against her rib cage, vied with the lust clenching her stomach, heating her pussy.

Exhaling, she forced herself to meet Xavier's impassive stare. How did he do it?

How did he turn his emotions on and off like a faucet?

One moment he held her, caressed her with so much passion need had overwhelmed her. And in the next he coldly studied her as if he hadn't palmed her sex and moaned into her mouth. How many nights had she lain awake dreaming of his kiss, of his hard, powerful body covering hers? She shivered. Too many to count.

Part of her—the part she allowed free only in the darkest hour of night—secretly thrilled at the idea of discovering what it meant to be his lover...of finally learning how he made love. Slow and tender? Fast and fierce? Did he gently guide a woman into ecstasy with whispered assurances and soft praise? Or did he catapult her into rapture, pushing the limits of her sensuality until she exploded in a hard, cataclysmic break? She bit the inside of her mouth, swallowed the moan welling in her throat.

After Joshua's death, she'd given up the dream of finding out. Now she had the chance...but at what cost? Accepting his offer reduced her to a prostitute. Yes, her submission would save the community center. But regardless of the altruistic reason, she had agreed to trade her body for money. Resentment tangled with regret. Xavier had blackmailed her for what she would have freely given him—had *yearned* to give him for years.

Pride demanded she tell him to shove the bargain up his ass. She could find other means to save the center. And need whispered at last she would know the heat and warmth of his skin sliding against hers. Know if his eyes burned bright with passion or darkened as desire rose. Know how his cock would stretch her pussy...fill the emptiness.

And after the passion cooled, in those quiet moments when the sweat dried on their skin and their racing pulses returned to normal, she'd find out if he would hold her close, her ear pressed to his heart. If he would caress her back, murmur loving words, or brush his lips over hers softly, so softly...

She pressed the back of her hand to her mouth as if she could imprison the taste of him between her lips.

Eyes that had been coolly assessing went arctic as they narrowed on the gesture. She dropped her arm and in her mind hit rewind then play, viewing her action through his eyes. *Damn.* From Xavier's point of view, it may have appeared as if she was wiping his kiss away.

"Don't worry," he said, the soft tone at odds with the cold fury burning in his jeweled gaze. "You have seven days to get accustomed to my mouth. Believe me, I plan to have it on you often enough."

Anger swirled in her belly, hot and welcome. The reminder of his devil's bargain erased the shame, the pain...the desire.

"But the week hasn't started yet," she growled. "And that kiss is the only freebie you'll receive."

His lips straightened into a grim slash and the harsh lines of his face hardened into an even more forbidding mask.

She paused, blinked. What? He didn't appreciate being reminded of his own terms?

She silently snorted. *Ridiculous.* After all, *he* was extorting *her.*

"Be at my house by six o'clock Saturday evening or I'll assume you've changed your mind about our agreement and my check will remain in my account. Do we understand each other?"

"Perfectly." Not trusting herself to remain in the same room with him any longer, she turned, stalked the small distance to the door and exited.

Let the countdown begin.

CHAPTER THREE

"As soon as he was gone, Beauty sat down in the great hall and fell a crying likewise…for she firmly believed Beast would eat her up that night."—Beauty *and the Beast*

"I am so screwed…and not in a good way."—Gwendolyn Sinclair

Two and a half hours.

One hundred and fifty minutes.

And Gwendolyn prayed the entire ride as her stomach pitched and heaved, every curve and dip in the road like a lunch-defying loop on a roller coaster. Sweat beaded on her forehead and coated her palms. Her slippery skin slid on the steering wheel as if it were the last life preserver on the Titanic.

"I can do this," she murmured the mantra. "Only a little farther to go. I can do this." Her stomach chose that moment to lurch hard and the ginger ale she'd purchased at the last stop surged. With a couple of desperate swallows, she coaxed the swell of liquid back down her throat, but not before it left behind an acidic burn on her esophagus. "Oh God, I can do this."

Minutes later, the sign for Great Barrington came into view and hope that the hellish trip would soon be over momentarily eased the debilitating queasiness. According to Xavier's e-mailed instructions, he lived right outside of the town. Even trepidation over what awaited her at the end of this drive—Xavier, a week of indentured-love servanthood—couldn't compete with the flood of relief.

In just a few more minutes, she could pass out in blessed oblivion.

At another time, she would have appreciated at the grand elegance of the historical First Congregational Church of Great Barrington. Marveled over the beauty of the Berkshires in the golden-and-auburn glory of fall. But with her raging fever and her gut threatening to turn inside out, the forest's natural splendor failed to impress. She needed a toilet or a bed—and it didn't matter which came first.

But as she coasted past the town's limits and the GPS chirped the number of miles before arriving at her destination, mortification returned with a vengeance. A tight knot coiled deep in the pit of her stomach. Images of the night in the study flashed through her mind. Like a video complete with audio, she viewed herself clinging to Xavier, arching into his kiss, grinding against his cock. *Hell.* She grimaced. It shamed her how easily he'd aroused her body. Five minutes with him and her nipples had beaded into tight points, her palms had prickled with the need to stroke his golden skin and her clit pulsed in a wild rhythm. As primed as she'd been, his one touch had almost catapulted her into nirvana.

Heat unrelated to her fever flamed her neck and cheeks. She wouldn't have been surprised to find third-degree burns blistering her face. Even now as her sex clenched in memory, arousal and guilt assailed her. Arousal because just the recollection of his caress dampened her panties—again. And guilt for the same reason.

This arrangement had nothing to do with love or even affection. Thinking back on the man she'd encountered several nights ago, she didn't believe he *liked* anyone. Himself included.

Xavier had transformed from the warm, funny man she'd known over half her life. His father's death and fiancée's defection had shriveled his heart, stealing his gentleness and kindness along with them. She should hate him for using her passion for the community center as hostage. That he would take advantage and exploit her desperation illustrated just how little of the man she'd grown up with remained.

And yet as much as she wanted to introduce her toe to his family jewels, the desire to pull him close, hold and comfort him, outweighed her anger.

Xavier's vitality and beauty had always captivated her—like a beautiful exotic bird she could admire yet never touch. Not until she'd grown older did she realize the vitality he emanated was an innate sensuality that blazed from within like a torch. And at some point, fascination had transcended to love and a terrifying need.

Her love and desire for Xavier was her secret...and shame.

Joshua had been safe—her best friend, a kind man and considerate lover. The stability he'd offered was the exact antithesis of the unreliable and emotional volatility of her mother. He'd been her haven. She'd never doubted she'd been first in his heart, in his love. His devotion had given her a security, an elusive sense of worth that had been missing from the time she'd been old enough to understand her mother had begrudged her every breath. Even when she'd recognized her love and desire for Xavier, the frightening power of it made her cling tighter to Joshua. Xavier scared her...or rather her need for him scared her. And even as her teenage attraction for the elder St. James brother deepened to a very adult desire, too many years of being Renee Sinclair's unwanted, unloved child kept her devoted to Josh.

And she had been devoted—even as she worshipped his godlike older brother. Xavier St. James had been a mesmerizing, barely contained blaze while Josh had been a warm, comforting fire in a hearth. Though beautiful, Xavier represented a risk she hadn't been prepared to face.

But this precarious balancing act had all come crashing down in the most horrific way. Her unfaithfulness of the heart had driven Joshua to his death when she'd finally, after years of living a lie, gathered the courage to confess she couldn't marry him. She hadn't mentioned Xavier, but Joshua had known. And she hadn't denied his accusations.

Gwendolyn had betrayed Joshua...and sent him to his death. She released a tremulous breath.

The burden of loving one brother and lying to the other had weighed on her until she could no longer look at herself in the mirror...or bear to meet Joshua's gaze. She'd convinced herself the fascination with Xavier would fade. What she had with Joshua was stable, lasting. But by the night of their wedding rehearsal dinner, she could no longer lie to herself or him. She waited until their guests left his parents' home and broke their engagement.

He'd seen through the flimsy excuses she'd given and she'd realized then Joshua suspected her true feelings for his older brother.

He exploded, but before she could respond, he had stormed out. Hours later, Xavier had arrived at her door to deliver the news of his brother's death. Joshua had wrapped his car around a telephone pole. She had fallen apart in Xavier's arms, knowing it had been her fault.

Her love for one brother had killed the other.

Perhaps her quick capitulation to Xavier's extortion was her means of penance. Penance for a love that refused to abate. Atonement for the need urging her to be with Xavier and snatch up the scrap of time their deal allotted.

"Turn left here. You have arrived at your destination," the GPS announced cheerily. Oh shut up. What are you so damn happy about?

Her stomach executed a flip worthy of a perfect ten. Bile roared up her digestive tract, scalded her trachea and played handball with the back of her throat. She whimpered as the white elegant marker for Xavier's house came into sight. *Oh, thank God.* Nerves tap-danced under her clammy skin, but the anxiety over beginning her service as Xavier's temporary mistress paled in comparison to her desperate gratification of finally arriving at her destination without puking in the car. She slapped her left turn signal even though the road behind her was empty of traffic and turned onto the narrow lane.

Besides, if she died from the plague twisting her insides into a pretzel then she wouldn't have to worry about being Xavier's sex slave for a week.

"Oh. Wow," she breathed. Her foot eased off the accelerator and the car slowed to a crawl as the sprawling home came into view.

Good Lord. This place differed from her small, West Roxbury apartment like the majestic mountains contrasted with Boston's steel giants.

A quintessential New England farmhouse greeted her, with a wide, spacious front porch and an emerald green lawn that seemed to stretch for miles. Out her side window, a fence as pristine white as the house ran the length of the driveway. Several elegant horses grazed behind the barrier and their regal beauty momentarily distracted her from the nauseating twists of her stomach. A city girl, she'd never had the opportunity to be around the animals much less ride one. They were beautiful.

Shaking her head, she pressed the gas pedal, continued up the long lane and soon pulled to a stop in front of the house. She shoved open the door and spilled out of the front seat. Every ounce of her strength and concentration was poured into covering the

space from the car to the front door. In reality, the distance was most likely a couple hundred feet, but it yawned to the size of a football field with each shuffling step.

Finally she climbed the steps and knocked on the door. *I made it.* She sighed. But the respite was short-lived. Nausea cramped her insides and a wave of darkness swamped her. It faded almost immediately, but the calling card of unconsciousness left her reeling on her heels and gold sparks twinkling in her peripheral vision. *Oh shit. I'm not going to make it.*

One of the front red double doors opened. She stared up at Xavier through a dim veil of misery. Yet even her abject suffering didn't detract from the potency of his sexual magnetism. Dammit.

He arched a dark-brown eyebrow. "Congratulations. You made it without a second to—" He frowned and the sarcasm melted from his tone to be replaced by confused irritation. "You look like shit."

"You charmer, you," she whispered. And then her world crashed to black.

* * * * *

She met Jesus.

And he was hot. Like gorgeous hot. Was that sacrilegious?

Must be, because He'd tossed her blasphemous ass into hell. And God—did one call on God when roasting in hell?—she was *burning up.* The flames licked and roasted every part of her body. Tears stung her eyes as she flipped to her left side. So this was how Joan of Arc had felt...

Wait. Not hot. Cool. Refreshing coolness. She cried...blubbering like a person who'd been redeemed from infinity as Satan's bitch. Maybe she hadn't been condemned to eternal damnation after all. Everyone knew there was no ice water in hell. How many times had her mother warned her of that?

God—she could call on him now, right?—the bracing cold on her skin was wonderful. Must be back in heaven.

And Jesus was still a hottie.

* * * * *

Gwendolyn fought to lift her eyelids. When had they been glued

29

shut? After several more seconds, she won the battle and a bright, hazy light immediately assaulted her eyes. Groaning, she tried to roll over...and remained still.

What the hell?

Bewildered, she sucked in a breath as anxiety crept into her chest like a stealthy thief. She attempted to move again and this time shifted to her side, but not without a lot of effort and heavy breathing. Jeez. Her breath rushed in and out of her nose and her muscles whined as if she'd just completed a marathon.

"So you're finally awake."

That voice blasted the confusing lethargy away. It all came crashing back. Xavier's proposition. Driving to his home.

Burning up...

Jesus?

Rolling to her back—which was a hell of a lot easier than moving to her side—she stared up into Xavier's gorgeous, scarred features. His sharp gaze examined her face as if tracing every line and dimension. She resisted the urge to skim her fingers over her skin. Not that she possessed the energy.

"How are you feeling?"

"Like I've been beaten like a runaway slave and hot pokers have been jammed into my eyes." Was that her grumpy response? *Sheesh.*

The corner of his full, sensual lips quirked before he turned toward the huge bay windows that allowed sunshine to spill across the blue comforter she huddled under. He dragged the curtains closed, shutting out the worst of the bright rays, and the fascinating play of muscles between his shoulder blades snagged her attention.

"Better, Kunta?"

"Much," she grumbled. *Smart ass.* "Thanks. What happened?"

"You've been sick with fever for two days."

She gaped at him. Her mind reeled. She'd arrived in Great Barrington on Saturday evening. And Sunday...Sunday... She frowned. What the hell happened to Sunday?

"That's impossible," she protested.

"The doctor has been here three times since Saturday night." He arched an eyebrow as if daring her to object again. "If your fever hadn't broken yesterday afternoon, he was going to have you admitted into the hospital."

"But *I* went to the doctor and all I had was a twenty-four-hour virus."

Xavier crossed his arms. "When did you do that?"

Gwendolyn dropped her gaze to the blanket. He would ask that. "Friday," she mumbled.

Apparently he didn't just own the eyes of a hawk, but the ears of one too. "Friday?" he repeated, narrowing his gaze. "You were sick since Friday and still drove up here feverish on Saturday?" His arms dropped and his hot glare pinned her to the bed like a butterfly on a corkboard. "You fucking fainted on my doorstep, Gwen." She flinched at the quiet menace in his dark accusation. "If you had passed out behind the wheel instead of in my arms, you could have been seriously hurt. Or worse." Xavier stalked closer. Tension corded his body and his hands balled into tight fists at his sides. "Why the hell didn't you call and tell me you were sick?"

"You wouldn't have believed me," she shot back, irritation rising and infusing her body with enough strength to struggle to sitting. Weakness be damned. She wouldn't spend another second lying flat on her back while he towered over her like a stern parent lecturing a recalcitrant child. "What are you so angry about, Xavier? I arrived here on the designated day by the designated time." All she contained in her arsenal to battle him with was the derision in her voice and she wielded it like a broadsword. "What? Are you mad because you've lost two days off your precious bargain? I humbly apologize that my fever cockblocked."

Xavier stiffened. Something…hurt?…flickered in his eyes before a glinting fury followed fast on its heels. He scowled so darkly, his scar whitened and she fought not to shrink into the pillows. *Hurt?* She scoffed. Must have been the residual effects of the fever. The mountain of stone looming over her could never experience a human emotion like pain.

"That's it exactly," he growled. "You have no idea how close you came to being fucked while you were delirious." He skewered her with one last disgusted glare before sharply spinning and stalking across the room. He gripped the doorknob and yanked the door open, pausing only long enough to bark, "Call whoever it is you need to notify about your stay being extended since I won't be able to collect for at least another two days. I believe in getting my money's worth." He slammed the door behind him.

Gwendolyn gaped, the echo of wood cracking against wood

31

ringing in her ears.

Whoa. She replayed their conversation in her head. What did he have to be angry—

Ah damn. She wanted to smack herself in the forehead, but her head ached already. How could she have been so stupid? So obtuse? *If you had passed out behind the wheel instead of in my arms, you could have been seriously hurt. Or worse.*

Of course. He'd lost both his brother and father in car accidents. Even if he didn't care for her, the fact she could have been hurt driving to his home because of their deal would have affected him. He probably feared car crashes like most people feared snakes or heights. She sighed. And she'd accused the man of being a horny asshole.

The only asshole in the room had been her.

* * * * *

Xavier lifted his hand to the gold doorknob of Gwendolyn's room. And paused. A low hum of anger simmered deep in his gut, but at least it had cooled from the inferno that had raged when he'd left her room earlier. Hours had passed before his fury had settled to a slow heat. During that time, the doctor had come and gone, he'd had a lunch tray sent up to her while she napped and he'd managed a few hours of work. Yet not until an hour ago had he dug past the bullshit and his offended pride to the heart of the reason cowering behind his anger. Gwendolyn had every right to be suspicious of his motives. Hell, since the moment they'd reunited, he'd rebuffed her, blackmailed her, and then shoved his hand between her thighs.

Yeah, he'd done a bang-up job of bolstering her confidence in his character.

Yet acknowledging she had reason to suspect his concern didn't lessen the sting. Once upon a time she had been free with her smiles and affection. Before Josh's death six years ago and his father's just this past year. Before the disfiguring scar. Before his life had gone to shit.

Prior to the car accident, he would have never considered himself vain or self- absorbed. His appearance and lifestyle had been things he'd taken for granted. It wasn't until after the bandages had been removed and people stared as if he belonged in a cage like a sideshow freak—and those he'd believed friends avoided him like the clap—

he'd realized how much his life had revolved around those superficial aspects. His eyes had been opened to how shallow his life had been…as well as the people in it.

The truth didn't prevent him from being bitter as hell, though.

With a muttered curse, he twisted the knob and opened the bedroom door. Gwendolyn reclined on a mound of pillows, her unruly curls a bright halo around her head.

God, he loved her hair. Even when Josh was alive, her soft, springy curls had been a source of erotic dreams. He'd envisioned snagging the spirals in his fist as he dragged her head back for his mouth. Or imagined the soft slide of them over his chest and stomach as she tongued a path to his cock. Or dreamed of wrapping the curls around his flesh.

He'd never fantasized about fucking his ex-fiancée's hair, for Christ's sake.

He stepped into the room and closed the door behind him. Gwendolyn's lashes lifted at the muted click. Her dark gaze locked with his. Though still dulled by her bout with illness, the sharpness in her blatant scrutiny threatened to peer too deep, see too much. He turned away.

"Dinner is almost ready," he murmured, crossing the room and pausing at the foot of the bed. "I thought you might like a bath before you eat."

Her delighted sigh made him swivel his head to face her. Breath trapped in his throat, he thrust his hands in the front pockets of his pants to keep from reaching out to her. Here was a woman who did not take life for granted. Not when something as simple as a bath caused her lashes to lower and the corners of her soft mouth to tilt in a grin of hedonistic bliss. His heart hammered and he released his pent-up breath. It eased the drumming in his chest, but did jack shit for the pounding in his cock. He longed to see her cat-who-just-ate-the-cream smile as he rose from between her spread thighs, after she'd just come on his tongue.

"I would give you my firstborn child, Rumpelstiltskin."

His spurt of amusement caught him off guard. Laughter had been in short supply for a long while and the tickle of humor was strange. How…sad. Had his existence become so solitary, his bitterness so entrenched, joy was an alien experience?

He cleared his throat and tugged on the bedcovers. "Not

necessary, since any child of yours would probably inherit your 'hell on wheels' gene."

"I was precocious." Gwendolyn scowled at his snort, eased to sitting and gingerly swung her legs over the side of the bed. The large T-shirt he'd clothed her in bared smooth brown thighs and calves to his starved gaze. With herculean effort, he tore his stare away from her lovely skin, but the image stayed emblazoned in his mind.

With more care and gentleness than he would have believed himself capable of, he grasped her upper arm and helped her stand. After two bedridden days, her legs trembled and a slight tremor traveled up her body to the slender, fine-boned hand clutching his forearm. Muttering a curse, he bent his knees and hooked an arm beneath her knees while the other supported her back. He straightened with Gwendolyn in his arms, pressed to his chest.

Her squawk of surprise echoed in his ear as she flung her arms around his neck as if she dangled from a great precipice instead of several feet in the air. He rolled his eyes even as he surrendered to a small grin.

"Calm down, Gwen," he said.

"What are you doing?" she ranted. "You can't carry me. I'm too heavy."

"Don't I know it. I think I may've slipped a disk." He grunted and grinned wider at her outraged gasp. Truthfully, in spite of her height, she was a negligible weight in his arms. If she realized how much he savored the crush of her breasts against his chest and the press of her soft thighs over his arm, she would have demanded he lower her to floor. Good thing his parents had raised a man intelligent enough not to mention the obvious.

Her protests continued into the spacious bathroom and didn't end until he lowered her to the top of the closed toilet lid.

"I can't believe you did that," she grumbled as he turned to the large, Jacuzzi-style bathtub and twisted the faucets. Water gushed out and filled the bottom of the tub in seconds. He wiggled his fingers under the steady stream, testing the warmth. Satisfied, he whirled on his heel and exited. It required only moments to gather a fresh pair of pajama bottoms and one of the tank tops she'd packed, along with the vanilla-scented shampoo and conditioner. When he returned to the bathroom, her scowl transformed into a delighted smile as her eyes lit on the articles in his hands.

"Are you ready?" He placed the clothes and bottles on the counter and stepped forward.

"Yes." Her wide brown eyes dipped to the floor before lifting to meet his once again. "Xavier, I can't, um, get undressed with…" She fluttered her fingers in his direction.

He grasped what she had a hard time voicing and suppressed the automatic objection tickling his throat. Hell, who did she think had bathed her and changed her sweat-drenched clothes for the past two days? The need to protect her from further injury warred with her determination to preserve her pride. He sighed. She was weak, uncertain and vulnerable. He understood her need to have a tight rein over even the smallest detail when everything else was spinning out of control.

"I will be right outside the door. Call me if you feel the slightest bit faint or sick and I'll come right in. Promise me?" Her relieved nod was immediate and, though he would've rather been beside her in the room, her grateful smile turned him into enough of a sucker to leave and shut the door behind him.

He wedged his shoulder against the doorjamb and waited, listening for any sign of distress on the other side of the door. When a soft splash followed by a tired sigh reached him, he released his own gust of breath. And relaxed.

The muffled sounds of her bathing became a form of exquisite torture. Thanks to her illness, he knew exactly what beauty awaited in the other room. Their forced intimacy had stripped away any barrier of modesty. Animal lust had clawed at his gut even as fever had raged through her lovely body. Of course he hadn't sunk so low on the moral barometer he'd molested her, but it would have taken an act of God to keep him from imagining those luscious curves writhing under him in a heat not associated with illness.

Snorting with disgust, he grasped the knob and entered the bathroom again. "Dammit, Xavier!" Gwendolyn gasped. Water splashed and he glimpsed smooth brown shoulders before she disappeared beneath the rippling surface of the water. As if her hands and the small square cloth he'd left her to bathe with would hide her body from him if he stepped to the tub's edge.

Shit. He stifled a moan and wheeled toward the counter. His heart and cock throbbed from the brief flash of flesh alone. She had been in his home, sick for three days. *Sick, you perverted piece of shit.* Yes, she was on the mend, but she remained as weak as a newborn foal. Gwendolyn needed care, not out-of-control lust. He inhaled and willed the arousal away. Splashes of water and her sputtered curses filled the room as she came up for air. *Good.* He exhaled, the breath slow and even. *It's all goo*— Fuck, he wanted her. He closed his eyes, grabbed the shampoo bottle and held on as if it were the last paddle on shit's creek.

"Calm down, Gwen," he said soothingly. *Hello, kettle. I'm pot.* "I'm just going to wash your hair." When he opened his eyes, the gaze that met his in the mirror gleamed bright green with desire and anticipation. The shadows of fear and longing for something other than her body that lurked behind his arousal—he ignored those. He turned with the shampoo in hand and faced her glare.

"I can wash my own hair," she said, drawing her knees to her chest and encircling them tight with her arms.

"You could," he agreed and settled his hip on the wide lip of the tub. "But I'm going to."

"Fascist," she snapped as he flicked the cap up.

Xavier snorted and shifted more of his weight onto the tub's ledge.

"That's not what you called me two nights ago." He leaned forward, removed the cloth band she'd use to constrain her hair in a high ponytail and drizzled a large dollop of clear vanilla-scented shampoo in his palm. "Then I was Jesus."

"I did not—" He tunneled his fingers into the thick strands, scrubbing his palms over her scalp, and her protest morphed into a long, satisfied moan. He smiled and continued the firm massage. "Oh my God, that feels good," she sighed.

The smile vanished from his lips as he conjured images of her uttering the same words, arching over him as she took his cock in her sex. Or of him savoring that same sweet flesh with his mouth.

"Xavier?"

The soft voice dragged him back to the present. His fingers had stilled mid-stroke and Gwendolyn stared at him over her shoulder.

"Sorry," he murmured, the word husky as thoughts of having her wet, tight sheath surrounding him and the sugary spice of her on his tongue flooded his mind. "Lean your head back so I can rinse the shampoo out."

As he stood and removed the detachable showerhead from its

anchor, she snickered. "I didn't really call you Jesus, did I?"

He couldn't prevent the grin from stretching his lips any more than he could have tamped down his lust. Water poured from the spigot in a thunderous rush before he twisted another knob and the downpour switched to a steady stream from the showerhead. He waved his fingers under the water to test its warmth. Satisfied with the temperature, he lifted the nozzle to Gwendolyn's hair. The loose honey-colored curls darkened to caramel under the spray and tightened into the corkscrews that had always fascinated him. Still did.

"Yes, 'fraid so." He would have added she'd also poked his chest and called him a lumpy but warm blanket as she'd burrowed closer to him, but revealing that bit of information would involve explaining he'd slept in the bed with her. Yeah, not the best time to expose how intimate they'd actually become over the past two days.

"I don't see why my supposed divinity surprises you," he said, setting the showerhead on the side of the tub. "I delivered your sweet ass out of so many scrapes when we were younger, I might as well be your savior."

Her laughter bounced off the tiled walls. "You're exaggerating, Xavier. I may have been curious and…*active*, but I wasn't a terror."

He snorted his disbelief and poured more shampoo into his hand before rubbing it in her hair. Again Gwendolyn emitted a small moan and the low, dark sigh rippled down his cock. His fingers tensed momentarily before resuming the massage.

"What about the time you scheduled a fight for three o'clock behind the community center with the biggest eleven-year-old God had ever created, and I had to break it up before that girl handed your ass to you in a sling?"

"She was a bully."

"And the time I had to drive out in the middle of the night to pick up you and your girlfriends on the side of the road because your car broke down on the way home from sneaking into that all-male revue?"

"A rite of passage?"

"And we can't forget about the streaking incident in college. Not only did I have to go down to the police station and bail you out, but I also had to promise all sorts of things to the dean of students so she would agree not to suspend you from school."

"You did take one for the team that time, Xavier." She chuckled and leaned her head back for another rinse. Her grin stretched wide. "But at least she was pretty."

"She was at least fifty years old to my twenty-three and I had to dodge her phone calls for a year after our dinner," he growled and playfully tugged her hair.

Her exaggerated yelp drew a rusty laugh from him.

"I wouldn't have made it through college without you." She closed her eyes as he threaded his fingers through her thick, sodden hair, ensuring all the shampoo had been washed out. "Sacrifices notwithstanding, the phone calls to check in on me, unexpected visits to cart me to dinner, even help with my papers and exams..." She shook her head. "You were the best friend I had. I never admitted this before, but when Joshua announced he was attending Rhode Island University and leaving me in Boston, I was scared as hell. For the first time since we were kids, I faced being alone. But with you there, I wasn't by myself. I've never thanked you for that. I'm sure you had better options than spending evenings with your younger brother's girlfriend." She lifted her lashes and he stared down into her dark-brown gaze. The laughter had disappeared from her voice and the smile had faded from her lips.

"I missed you." Her quiet admission resonated in the still room. "After Joshua returned and you stopped coming around as much, I missed you."

The steady spill of water from the showerhead filled the silence. Like a coward, he glanced away, switched the nozzle off and twisted the faucets.

"Joshua asked me to look after you while he was away. When he graduated and came home, my end of the bargain had been fulfilled." He rose and reattached the apparatus. The explanation revealed half the truth. But how could he confess he'd purposely stayed away once his brother returned because the resulting jealousy and possessiveness had confused and disturbed him?

At some point, he'd come to think of Gwendolyn as his, had resented Joshua's homecoming and what he'd viewed as his younger brother usurping his place in her life. The antipathy and envy had horrified him so he'd placed distance between the two of them until he could occupy the same space as her and not feel...cheated.

"You and your bargains," she murmured and rested her chin on her drawn-up knees. He paused, arm outstretched toward a towel hanging on the wall rod. If anger had laced her tone, he could have shaken her accusation off. No, irritation wouldn't have touched him, but the sadness in her solemn voice knocked at a conscience he'd believed silenced long ago.

"Gwen—"

"If you leave the towel on the tub, I can manage. Thank you for washing my hair."

An instinctive protest rose up in him, but he squashed it and lifted the towel from the bar.

"I'll get dinner for you." Placing the cloth on the edge of the tub, he studied the long elegant line of her naked back another moment before pivoting and leaving the room. As he closed the door and crossed to the hallway, he didn't know whether he was thankful for or regretted her interruption. *Thankful.* His fingers curled into a fist. *Definitely thankful.* The words he may have said would have only embarrassed them both.

Because, really…who could care for a beast?

CHAPTER FOUR

"Welcome Beauty, banish fear, you are queen and mistress here. Speak your wishes, speak your will, swift obedience meets them still."—Beauty and the Beast

"I sleep with one eye open…and the other one is only napping."—Gwendolyn Sinclair

Gwendolyn swung open the frosted-glass shower door and stepped free of the steamy cubicle. The steady drum of the water had loosened her muscles and eased the faint aches remaining from her bout of illness. She sighed, whipped a towel from the rack and rubbed it over her damp skin. For the first time in days, she felt human.

Good thing too.

Her reprieve was over.

Tuesday and Wednesday had passed in a hazy blur of naps, medicine and more naps. Xavier had been as solicitous as he'd been since she'd woken Monday. Nothing in his actions or tone had hinted at what thoughts transpired behind his mask of pleasantness. No, he'd been the perfect Florence Nightingale. Yet heated speculation glittered in his emerald gaze. If his fingers grazed her thighs when he set meal trays on her lap, tension invaded his muscles.

Now it was Thursday evening and her nerves danced a rumba that would have made Patrick Swayze proud. If Xavier had attempted to keep his anticipation under wraps the days before, he had abandoned the pretense today. Arousal had been stamped on his features, thickened his voice and set his gaze on fire. Not to mention the hard ridge of his cock a hazmat suit couldn't hide.

She would be a hypocrite if she denied the hunger excited her. God, it did. With a capital, bold, font size seventy-two "E". She just wished the circumstances were different. That he hadn't used her love for the community center and his wealth as hostage to compel her compliance. That he didn't want her only because he believed no other woman would have him. Out of all the wishes, the last one stung the most. No, she didn't possess the beauty, status or silver spoon his ex-fiancée and the women of his acquaintance did, but she wasn't a damn booby prize.

Now if her pussy would just get on the same page as her pride. Unfortunately the two had completely different agendas.

Her sex swelled and clenched whenever she was within feet of him. Hell, if she envisioned him—the hard body, sensual unsmiling mouth, hooded green eyes, beautiful face and tragic scar—her pulse slammed into overdrive and blood pounded through her veins and pooled in her clit, engorging the tiny muscle to the point of madness. He was a fever no aspirin could alleviate.

A shiver scuttled over her skin as she drew on her panties, pajama bottoms and tank top. After folding the towel, hanging it back on the rod and tidying the bathroom, she grasped the doorknob and twisted. The hour had to be almost nine. Maybe he'd changed his—

Oh. My. God.

Shock crashed into her, knocking the breath from her lungs. Barely inside the bedroom, she stilled like a deer trapped by a stalking predator. Every fiber of her being was claimed by the silent man sprawled on the wingback chair across the room.

Air rushed back into her lungs with a painful whoosh as if her body had fallen asleep, and blood flooded her veins with needles of awareness, trepidation...and anticipation.

She couldn't tear her gaze away from him. A black V-neck sweater molded to his wide shoulders and broad chest. Dark pants encased his long legs and she shivered at the barely contained power emanating from his motionless form. He resembled a panther. Sleek. Sensual. Elegant. And with his thick golden-brown hair drawn back to his nape and the scar visible—dangerous.

"What are you doing here?" Outrage. Outrage would have been

more effective than the mortifying breathlessness.

"You're my houseguest," he said and the tone stroked over her like a luxurious fur over naked skin. Rich. Soft. Sensual. "I came to check on you. How are you feeling?"

"Fine. Fever-free." She bared her teeth in a smile, adding a casual shrug for good measure. He had one purpose for entering her room tonight. If Xavier's intention was to check on her health, he would've knocked and turned on the light. No, tonight she fulfilled her end of the bargain.

"Good. I brought you a gift." He nodded toward the bed and the small pink box on top of the light-blue quilt. "Open it," he said softly, but brooking no argument.

Sit, Boo-boo, sit. Good dog. She scowled, but moved from the doorway and edged closer to the bed. She stared at the box as if it were one of Australia's deadly dozen. The small pastel package was embossed with the name of a popular lingerie boutique. Her stomach plummeted even as her sex heated.

"Open it, Gwendolyn."

She jerked her gaze to him and just as quickly glanced away from the bold, intent scrutiny. Cowardice didn't sit well in her gut, but the alternative—revealing the arousal his jeweled stare ratcheted from flame to full-out conflagration—was a more foolhardy move. Already she shivered like the prey of the big cat he resembled. She was hunted, snared. And God, she wanted to be taken down.

Her fingers fisted before she consciously relaxed them and reached for the gift. It required little fuss to unwrap the present—just a tug on the ribbon and remove the lid. Inside, atop white tissue paper, rested pale-blue lace. Wary, she lifted the delicate material and it transformed into a tiny bra too flimsy to support a feather much less her breasts and a pair of miniscule panties that—

Oh hell, no! Her back stiffened and heat blasted her face. She couldn't see her cheeks, but she harbored no doubt she'd just debunked the myth that black people didn't blush.

She'd fortified herself for this evening. Yesterday morning when the doctor had declared her on the mend she'd assumed tonight would most likely be the commencement of her week as Xavier's lover. As "paramour" couldn't be included on her resume, she hadn't known what to expect. Darkness. Quick shedding of clothes. Sex under the covers. The dark part had been right on target, but this...

Again she dropped her gaze to the fragile material. Did he expect her to parade around for him? Place herself on display?

The hell she would.

"You must be kidding me," she blurted. "I can't." But his raised eyebrow assured her he wasn't and she would.

The crotchless underwear dangled from her finger as if mocking her. The bra she could deal with. It would barely conceal her nipples, but at least provided some cover.

But the panties...

"I won't put these on," she said and silently congratulated herself when the announcement didn't sound like the hysterical shriek reverberating in her head.

"Oh, but you will, Gwendolyn." Xavier contradicted her with a nod. "You seem to possess an affinity for those words—no, can't, won't. And I am constantly reminding you the time for choices and objections presented itself a week ago." He tsked. "I think you've forgotten the details of our arrangement. As soon as you decided to come to me, you agreed to submit your will to mine. You're here for my pleasure. And it will please me to see you in my gift." Lust thickened his deep voice, mirrored in his hooded green gaze. "Now put them on."

Anger swelled and wiped out her embarrassment. So the asshole from a week ago had reappeared, locking the man who had cared for her the past five days inside a carefully constructed prison of cold ruthlessness.

Helplessness fed her rage—helplessness because he was right. Once she arrived on his doorstep, she'd surrendered the right to object to his plans.

She crumpled the insubstantial material in her fist. Fine. She'd entered this devil's bargain with her eyes wide open. It wasn't enough she had to crawl to him and prostitute herself. Now he had to humiliate her too. Well, fuck him. She'd put on the bra and bits of lace he called panties. But she'd be damned if she'd cower in front of him. She whirled on her heel and stalked toward the bathroom door.

"Where are you going?"

She screeched to a halt and slowly turned, contempt burning a hole in her chest. "To the bathroom to put on your shi—*gift*."

"No." He shook his head. "You'll dress out here. In front of me."

"Fine," she gritted through clenched teeth. What had she

expected? Tenderness? Compassion? Seduction? In the secret depths of her heart, she'd hoped he would treat her as a lover and not as a body to dress, position how he wanted and screw. *Lovers.* She curled her lip. That term denoted intimacy. They would fuck. That was part of their bargain. Fucking and intimacy were two different animals. One involved surrendering her body. The other, her heart.

Maybe he noticed the clenching of her jaw or the tension threatening to snap her body in two, for a small half-smile curved his lips.

"That sounded nice, Gwendolyn, even if you didn't mean it." He tilted his head to the side and the tiny smile continued to play about his mouth. "Don't worry, though. By the time you leave here, no part of your body will remain a secret. Every inch of you will be touched, kissed, sucked," he lowered his lashes until only the barest hint of green remained visible under the thick fan, "and fucked by me."

Oh Jesus. Liquid fire gathered between her thighs. Her clit beat in time with her galloping pulse. No. No way could she be furious and *so damn turned on* at the same time.

"You're being crude on purpose."

"What?" he asked with a lift of his eyebrow. "Fucking is crude? Did none of your previous lovers wax poetic to you?"

"No," she snapped and, though it was fighting dirty, flung the next words at him anyway. "Josh didn't need to."

The temperature seemed to drop ten degrees with the stony, frigid silence that descended in the room. She wouldn't have been surprised if puffs of air clouded in front of her face. Xavier didn't move a muscle, yet she sensed the cold fury lying beneath his deceptively indolent façade. She drew in a tremulous breath. Yeah, that was the thing about fighting dirty—a person sometimes ended up grimy.

"Don't bring him into this bedroom again," he warned and she shivered. "If you insist on dragging my sainted brother between us, then I'll enjoy reminding you who it is fucking you. Now," he said, propping his elbows on the arms of the chair and steepling his fingers under his chin, "you might want to quit stalling. I'm growing bored. And if I walk out of here, I'm not coming back."

Bored? Yeah, right. Even the dim lighting couldn't conceal the long length of his cock pressed against his pants leg like an iron rod. At the last moment, common sense prevailed and she abstained from hurling his lie back in his face. She just had to get through this night. Bottom line—she'd accepted the terms of his bargain. Now it was put up or shut up.

She retraced her steps to the bed and cast the lingerie on top of the blanket. With economical, quick movements, she tugged the tank over her head and dropped it to the floor. Fury kept the embarrassment of standing bare-chested before him at bay.

"Slow, Gwendolyn. Go slower."

And that fast her anger evaporated under the heat of lust. His lust. Her lust. Or maybe the arousal-thickened voice issuing the command inflamed her so the hunger no longer belonged to solely him or her, but to them both.

She hooked her thumbs in the waistband of the cotton bottoms and eased them over her hips, down her legs. His harsh intake of breath as she stepped from the puddle of material shot a lance of desire to her clit and her pussy spasmed, spilling creamy warmth over her folds.

"Keep going, baby," he whispered.

Xavier's rapt attention didn't waver as she repeated the process with the panties. He lowered his arms, tugged his belt loose. Captivated, she couldn't tear her gaze away as he lowered the zipper, reached inside his pants and freed his cock.

Oh God.

He was beautiful. And terrifying.

He encircled the base of the thick stalk and stroked up...and up. The motion employed use of his arm not just his wrist, and as he closed his fist around the fat head, she swallowed a whimper. It seemed impossible she could take the intimidating length inside her, but damn, she wanted to try. Even the bulbous head would stretch her wide.

Breathing deep, she reached for the bra. The small bit of blue lace fastened in the front and the scalloped edges concealed her nipples, but the dark areolas remained visible. She should have been mortified...moments ago she would have been. But the lust-filled grimace every time he stroked his flesh destroyed any vestiges of embarrassment. Even when she slid the crotchless underwear up her thighs and hips, she experienced no shame. Especially when his eyes narrowed on her exposed sex.

"Come here, Gwendolyn," he beckoned and the sensual note

drew her forward as if he were the last slice of chocolate cake at a Weight Watchers meeting. Tempting. Sinful. And dangerous. Except cake would be a threat to her hips and he endangered her spirit, her pride...her heart.

She paused between his spread thighs and Xavier released his cock to grip her hips. While she'd stood across the room, the heavy juice coating her swollen lips had been easy to conceal. Yet as he urged her to his lap and she straddled his thighs, the sexy lingerie hid nothing and he wouldn't miss the evidence of her desire.

His bright gaze bore into hers. An emotion flared in his eyes, there and gone before she could identify it. He lowered his lashes and the weight of his study caressed her like a physical touch.

"You're soaked." Fire scorched her face, shyness bumping aside need. She dipped her chin and the muscles in her thighs quivered as she shifted to conceal her bared sex.

"No," he whispered, his hard grip stilling her restless movement. "Don't ever hide your desire from me. I need to see it."

Before she could reply, Xavier dragged her forward until her pussy pressed against the base of his cock. Pleasure razed a path from her sex and blasted throughout her body before converging on the throbbing flesh between her thighs. Pure heat burned bashfulness away in a sprinkle of ash. She shuddered with hunger and bit her bottom lip, but couldn't hold back a whimper as her feminine folds parted under the pressure of the slow, erotic ride up his steel shaft.

She gripped the tense muscles of his upper arms. "Oh God."

The whimper became a soft cry as her clit bumped the hood of his cock head and small shocks of delight attacked the engorged button. Her sheath clenched and released in a hungry rhythm and she couldn't control the tight swivel of her hips. Xavier grunted beneath her and dug his fingers deeper into her hips. She repeated the motion, yearning to hear the carnal noise again. She was immediately rewarded as another groan rumbled in his chest.

With a growl, he wrenched the control from her and rolled her back down his cock. Then retraced the sensuous path. It should have embarrassed her, the slick path her pussy passed over his flesh. He hadn't touched her with his fingers, hadn't been inside her and yet she was as wet as if she'd experienced multiple orgasms. She had never known she was capable of becoming this sensual creature who didn't care if her juices coated his cock like a thick layer of icing. But no man—not even Joshua—had ever made her want with a fierceness rivaling a category ten hurricane.

"Shit, Gwen," he grated. He studied the sight of her swollen lips parted over his glistening shaft, released one hip and dipped his hand between her legs. She gasped as he swiped the clinging moisture from her folds with one finger and lifted it to his mouth. Xavier sucked the gleaming wetness.

Whose moan echoed in the room? His or hers? One of them emitted the needy sound. Maybe they both had. She sighed. The sight of him tonguing her taste from his finger could give her eye-gasms.

"Sweet." The word rumbled from his chest. His eyes glittered in the semi-darkness. "I've never tasted anything sweeter."

He gathered more of her essence and slowly painted her mouth. The gentle, tender touch wielded a different but no less overwhelming eroticism. The earthy scent drifted to her nose and she yielded to the instinctual urge to sweep the tip of her tongue over her damp lips. Desire had a flavor. Rich. Tangy.

"It's addictive," Xavier growled. He cupped the base of her skull in his large palm and hauled her forward, the sudden movement catching her off guard. Her hands flattened against his chest and his tongue captured her tiny surprised gasp as he licked the cream from her lips.

Oh damn.

She couldn't label the caress a kiss, but it jolted straight through her. The wet stroke reverberated in her breasts, abdomen and core. The taste of him. Wild. Fresh like the air after a spring rain and yet dark like a heavy sky right before a storm. *More.* Please, God, she wanted more.

"There won't be any ghosts in that bed tonight, Gwen. Not when your pussy is flowing like a fucking river. For me."

It had always been him. No one else, but him.

CHAPTER FIVE

"Tell me, do not you think me very ugly?"—Beauty and the Beast

"You can't bullshit a bullshitter."—Xavier St. James

"Look at me, Gwen." Xavier tightened his grip on her scalp and shook her head, emphasizing his command. He needed to see her eyes, to gaze into them and know his disfigurement didn't keep her from burning for him. The eyes and slick cream on his dick couldn't lie. Time crawled as she complied with his demand. She lifted her lashes and bleak shadows haunted the brown depths. But hunger smoldered there too. He ignored the sadness and concentrated on the desire. Not addressing the emotion made him a bastard, but if she admitted memories of his brother had caused the sorrow, he would go apeshit.

Inside he cringed at his selfishness, ashamed, but not enough to let her go. Not enough to grant her space and time to reconcile her feelings for the man she'd been on the verge of marrying. Joshua had been the love of her life—Xavier didn't even entertain the possibility of replacing him in her heart. He couldn't. Especially not now with his disfigured face, scarred body and damaged psyche. But Joshua was dead. And he was alive and needed Gwendolyn in a way his brother never had.

"Kiss me." The words rasped his throat, more an order than a plea. Her steady scrutiny unsettled him. Every self-protective instinct inside him screamed a warning to avoid her intent examination, but he didn't succumb. And God, did he want to elude the scalpel-like precision that seemed to peer beneath his skin and bone to the bitterness, rage and grief beneath. To the dark places he wasn't prepared for her to intrude.

"Kiss me, dammit," he growled. He tangled his fingers in the soft light-brown curls, intending to compel her obedience.

Then she leaned forward. And brushed her lips across his jaw. His chin. His lips.

Shock gripped him in its icy claws. The air froze in his lungs as again the soft touch of her kiss grazed his numb mouth. Such gentleness. Like a comforting hand in the dark. A tender whisper in the middle of howling winds. His grip in her hair slackened. His lips grew pliant under hers. And her taste—from her body and the sweet flavor of her soft breath—exploded onto his palate.

A groan originated from the ravenous, insatiable pit in his soul. He lunged forward and devoured her mouth. Plundered. Took. And, God help him, prayed he gave. But need rode him hard and furious and he couldn't tell.

He clutched her ass and shot up from the chair. Gwendolyn encircled his neck with her arms and wrapped her legs around his waist. He stumbled in the trek toward the bed when her tongue speared between his lips. Her bare, hot sex ground against his cock. Fuck, if she was this wet now how would she respond once he penetrated and filled her? His dick flexed. She would squeeze his flesh like a stingy fist and bathe him in her liquid fire at the same time.

His knees hit the edge of the mattress and, as he pitched forward, he shifted his hands to her back to cushion their fall. They tumbled to the bed, bounced once and then settled. Still he couldn't stop kissing her. Couldn't get enough of her.

"Xavier," she gasped.

Her chest heaved beneath him and the full breasts threatened to spill free of the thin lace. He levered back far enough to cup the firm flesh, freeing her of the insubstantial material. A sharp cry burst from her throat as he molded the mounds to his palms and dragged his thumbs across the tight, hard nipples. Like buttered cream topped with the sweetest, darkest berries. No country club or exclusive dining room he'd ever patronized could have offered a more exquisite treat.

He captured a pebbled tip with his lips and sucked it deep. Her scream came seconds before the sting of her nails bit into his scalp. Both were just as satisfying as the taut flesh he flicked with his tongue.

"Xavier, please," she pleaded, hips writhing.

He drew back and released the nipple with a soft, wet *pop*.

"Please what, baby?" he murmured. Unable to *not* touch her for any length of time, he rubbed his lips over the moist peak. Nudged it with the pointed tip of his tongue. "Talk to me, Gwen. Please what?"

"Suck me harder," she panted, fingers clutching his hair and tugging the strands from the band at his nape. He stiffened. Fear seized him and squeezed its merciless fist around his heart. For a moment, dread supplanted passion.

"Xavier? What's wrong?" He jerked his eyes to her face. A small frown furrowed her brow. What could he say? He dropped his gaze to the center of her chest. *I need you to look at my face so I can catch the first sign of disgust?* Evelyn had preferred his hair loose the few times they'd had sex after the accident. With the thick strands unbound, the scar had been hidden. He had allowed the pretense, so desperate to believe at least one thing remained constant in a world that had morphed into a cold, strange place in the span of one tragic night.

After he'd discovered Evelyn's affair and she'd left, blaming his disfigured face for the end of their relationship, he had refused to allow himself the luxury of deliberate ignorance. With his hair drawn back, no one could pretend the scar didn't exist—and he couldn't pretend to not see their horror.

"Xavier." She called his name again and released his head.

If possible, he stiffened further as her fingers neared his ruined cheek. In a flash of movement, he grasped both her wrists and pinned them to the bed on either side of her shoulders. Her sharp intake of breath ended on a strangled moan as he latched onto the nipple he hadn't yet feasted on, then sucked it hard and deep as she'd requested.

He became lost in her again, forgetting everything but the flesh in his mouth. Gwendolyn squirmed beneath his lashing tongue. The muscles in her arms tensed as she strained to free herself from his hold, but he held fast. And tortured both himself and her.

He turned from one breast to the other, tracing wide circles around her areolas before dragging his flattened tongue over the taut tips. Her cries spurred him on, encouraged him to score her beaded flesh with his teeth. He drew on the peaks so strongly, she dug her heels into the backs of his thighs and levered her hips from the mattress to stroke his cock with her pussy.

Fuck. That pussy.

The only thing capable of tearing him away from the fantasy of her breasts was the dream of savoring the sweet sex he'd only had the chance to palm. He slid down her body, lowering her bound arms to rest beside her hips. Gwendolyn's restless thrashing didn't deter him from planting damp kisses on her narrow rib cage, flat stomach and navel. Her intoxicating musk drifted to him and he rubbed his cheek over the smooth, soft skin of her abdomen.

Aside from the doctors who had sewn his face back together, the small caress to the raised scar was the first in three years. He indulged in one last pass over her skin before he lowered his head to the soaked triangle of curls between her legs and nuzzled the top of the dark nest.

Gwendolyn stilled as if in anticipation of his next touch. He didn't leave her in suspense.

At the first stroke of his tongue through her swollen folds, a cry exploded from her throat and her hips bucked so hard she dislodged him. With a growl, he released her wrists and tugged her hands toward her sex.

"Hold your pretty pussy open for me, Gwen," he directed, moving her fingers until she spread herself wide for his gaze and tongue. His mouth watered for a taste of the dark-pink glistening flesh and the hooded, engorged clitoris. "Don't let go." He wedged his shoulders under her spread thighs, then cupped and lifted her ass so the splayed lips were like an offering to his mouth.

And he gorged on her.

Skill and technique vaulted out the window as he delved in the dewy cleft. Cream filled his mouth and he swallowed as if she offered him the sweetest delicacy. He lapped and stroked, thrust and flicked with his tongue. He couldn't get enough. When he slid two fingers inside her pussy, the muscles clamped them like a vise. His cock jerked in response as if begging for the same tight, slick grip on his fingers. Damn. He panted, pressing a pursed kiss to her clit.

Gwendolyn twisted uncontrollably and her broken sobs

punctuated the room.

"Xavier." She reached for his head, but he jerked back before she could touch him. Both of her hands dropped to his shoulders. Confusion and a flash of hurt shadowed her eyes. Regret, sharp and hot, spliced through his chest. Arousal and passion should've been the only emotions inhabiting this room, not pain.

He snagged a wrist, captured and suckled her fingers and sipped the hints of her sweet cream from the fingertips. As he coiled his tongue and savored, he plied steady, short thrusts to her slit, dragging more evidence of her desire from the snug channel with each withdrawal. Her choppy breaths and the suck and release of her wet flesh filled his ears.

"Mmm..." he hummed, pulling her fingers free of his mouth. "Can you do something for me, baby?" He waited for her nod. "Touch yourself. Play with your clit."

"I-I can't," she stammered, eyes widening.

"Yes, you can." The cadence of his strokes slowed until they stilled. "Show me how you make yourself come in the darkest part of night. Show me how Gwen, the woman, likes to be touched when Gwendolyn, the community center director, disappears." He bent his head and nuzzled her curls, inhaled her scent and trapped the tangy aroma in his lungs. "I want to learn what pleases you."

She lowered her long lashes at his words and the dark fringe veiled her gaze.

"Look at me, baby," he said. When she complied, he placed a kiss to her fingertips and lowered them between her thighs. "It's just you and me. No one else. Anything goes in this bed. No shame. No embarrassment."

For a heartbeat of silence, she stared at him. Then she slid a hesitant caress over the swollen button. Then another. And one more. This time when her eyes closed, he didn't demand she reopen them. Pleasure tightened her delicate features, painted a lovely flush on her cheekbones.

"That's it, baby," he praised, breathing harsh. "Good girl." He shuddered and his ass tightened as he dry-humped the mattress, seeking a bit of relief for his throbbing cock. "Good girl," he rasped.

She circled the hard nub, the motions no longer tentative. Her hips followed the pace set by her touch and her other hand plucked at her taut nipple. Labored puffs of air escaped her parted lips and

Xavier couldn't believe how sensual—beautiful—she appeared.

"My turn," he whispered and picked up her erotic rhythm, finger-fucking her silken sheath with long, slow plunges. They worked in tandem, each slow thrust stoking the fire in his veins higher and hotter. With one hand plying her sex, he lifted the other to her neglected breast and pinched the tight peak. Once more her cries broke over him as her body twisted and rolled.

"Oh God," she screamed, face contorted into a mask of lust and need. "Finish me.

Oh God, finish me."

With a low raw moan, he deserted her breast to grip her hip. He lowered his head over her fingers, nudged them aside and closed his lips over her clit. And sucked— hard.

She came apart.

Spasms quaked through her body. Her pussy clamped down, imprisoning his fingers in the tight channel even as she bathed his hand in hot cream. Sharp nails bit into his scalp and he didn't bother to evade them. Even as she undulated beneath him, he continued to lap at her flesh. Her sobs gradually quieted to whimpers, and then pants. At length, she loosened her clasp on his head and her arms slumped to her sides.

Yet he couldn't resist sampling her one last time.

"Enough…please," she pleaded on the tail end of a moan and made a halfhearted attempt to push his head away.

He chuckled and offered her a small smile. "Not fucking likely."

Her juice coated his lips and her pussy quivered around his fingers, inflaming a hunger that incinerated his control. If he didn't get his cock inside her… Hell, he *needed* to get his cock inside her.

He jackknifed off the bed and strode to the bedside table and lamp. With a twist of his wrist, the room was plunged into darkness, alleviated only by the small amount of moonlight peeking through the gaps in the drawn drapes.

"Xavier?"

He ignored the question and surprise in her voice and whipped his sweater over his head. Once she touched him, she would figure out why he'd doused the light. After removing a small foil packet from his front pocket, he tossed his pants and underwear to the floor. Naked, he straightened, and his eyes had adjusted enough to the dark to drink her in like a thirsty man staring at an ice-old bottle of water.

Her sex, a shade darker than the shadows, drew his ravenous gaze. He'd just sipped from the intoxicating flesh between her thighs and he longed for more. A sliver of unease pierced his heart. If he was smart, he'd tell her to get dressed and walk out of this room. One time—one week—would never be enough to fill this ravenous need for her.

Xavier approached the bed, climbed onto it and crouched on his hands and knees over her. Arousal consumed him and he spared only a brief thought to the scars marring his chest and stomach. Her taste filling his mouth left no room for humiliation.

She stared up at him, her features loosened with pleasure—pleasure he'd placed there. Did she know what she'd given him tonight?

He mentally shook his head. How could she? How could she know by submitting to him so generously—so sweetly—she'd healed a part of his heart, his spirit? Until she'd come in his mouth and on his hand, he hadn't admitted to himself how much damage his ex-fiancée's rejection had wreaked.

Compounded by the wide berth most women cleaved around him, he'd doubted a woman could still want him...would see past his face and allow him close enough to bare the man who still existed beneath the scarred visage. And now, as she gazed at him in satiation instead of the horror he'd become accustomed to, a piece of his soul returned to him—battered, but strong and whole.

He lowered his head and brushed his lips over hers. Once. Twice. She circled his neck with her arms and drew him closer. Though blood raged through his cock, making it pound with insistence to be buried deep inside her tight sex, the kiss was soft, tender. Almost...loving. Her tongue tangled with his, sucked and caressed. Each moan and breathless sigh stroked his senses and shored up another crack in his heart.

"I need..." *You.* But he bit back the word that would reveal too much. "I need to be inside you, Gwen. Let me in."

She nodded and pressed a kiss to the corner of his mouth. "Yes."

Such a simple word yet it rocked his world, his soul. Leaning all his weight on one hand, he opened the other and offered the condom to her. "Put it on, baby."

With another nod, she ripped the package open and slid the latex free. Xavier studied her slim fingers with rapt fascination as she gripped the wide stalk and rolled the condom down his length. He growled as her touch grazed the sensitive, stretched skin. And when she released his cock, he almost demanded she return her hand to his flesh. It was that damn good.

His fingers circled the base of his erection and she sank her teeth into her bottom lip. The gesture struck him as anxious. As if she were nervous...

"How long has it been?"

She flicked her eyes up to him and her tongue peeked out to wet her lips. "Seven years."

Seven years. Shit. That would mean she'd been celibate since Joshua's death. No. His brother had been dead six years. So that meant... Surprise shot through him, followed by curiosity. But with his dick throbbing a primitive, hungry rhythm answers to his questions could wait. Fuck first. Answers second.

Shit. She'd reduced him to a caveman.

He inhaled a deep breath then released it through his nose. Right now he needed patience that had expired about the time she'd stripped out of her clothes. Somehow he had to find it, because getting inside her small pussy would require every ounce.

"Baby, you're very tight," he said. "We'll go slow and easy."

He rose and settled back on his heels. Heart speeding like a runaway train, he arrowed his cock toward her entrance. He palmed her slim thighs then eased them wider apart. His cock head parted her folds and penetrated her. Wet heat sizzled on his skin and he hissed. The sound almost covered her sharp intake of breath...almost.

Gwendolyn stared down her body to the point where they joined. Tension lined her face and her fists twisted the bedcovers. Her sex was like a tight rubber band squeezing the cock head so he could imagine how his dick stretched her. He splayed his fingers wide on the inside of her thighs. Gently, he smoothed his thumbs up and down the dark lips. God, how pretty they looked surrounding his cock. The visual conjured images of her mouth parted, sucking him in.

"Relax for me, baby," he coaxed and didn't try to contain the lust racing through him and thickening his voice. He pressed into her and gently massaged. "Your pussy feels so good," he murmured. "I want to sink into you, fuck you so hard and deep that my cock leaves an imprint."

Inch by inch, thrust by thrust, he settled his dick into her sex. He whispered praises each time her core stretched and accepted more of him, took him deeper. By the time he was fully seated inside her, sweat poured off them both. Xavier clenched his teeth against the burning pleasure. Her pussy hugged his cock like shrink-wrap, so snug...so damn right.

Gwendolyn writhed beneath him, her head bearing down on the pillow hard enough to cause an indentation. Back arched, hips rolling, she epitomized lust, arousal...need. The tiny muscles in her sex spasmed around his flesh, goading him to move. To fuck. Leaning forward, he planted a palm next to her head and clamped the back of one thigh, then shoved it back and high. It opened her pussy another impossible increment and his cock took immediate advantage, burrowing deeper.

"Talk to me, Gwen." He closed his eyes, locking his jaw. Fuck. Root to tip, she swallowed him. His balls pressed against the stretched opening and the pressure to the sac elicited a grunt of hunger. When he lifted his lashes, he met her fevered gaze. "C'mon, baby. Are you okay?"

"Yes." She clutched his arms in a desperate grip. "God, yes. Please move."

With a greedy rumble, he withdrew and surged into her hot sheath. Over and over he buried his cock in her pussy, riding like a man possessed—or obsessed. Gwendolyn met him thrust for thrust, stroke for stroke. Her long legs wrapped around his waist and held him in their tight embrace.

Enfolded in her arms and legs, both his palms next to her head, he succumbed to the animalistic lust tearing a hole in his gut and rushing up his cock. The headboard bounced against the wall, the clatter matching the tempo of each plunge. He reached between their bodies and brushed a caress over her clit before circling the engorged nub with hard, tight motions.

Gwendolyn stiffened, gasped then let out a broken cry as she shuddered in orgasm. Her pussy seized his cock seconds before convulsing in rhythmic quivers. The steady ripple of her muscles around his dick, the scrape of hard nipples against his chest and her scream of release echoing in his ears shoved him over the edge of oblivion. He plummeted into the fiery abyss like a phoenix, reborn in the flames of consuming passion.

The ecstasy lasted forever, but ended too soon. Before he was ready to return to sanity, he descended back to the bed, to the dim room. To...peace.

He opened eyes he didn't remember shutting. This woman, who'd given her flesh and passion so willingly, had gifted him with pleasure and precious forgetfulness. A soft sigh escaped his lips and, as Gwendolyn's eyes closed and she drifted to sleep, he placed a gentle kiss on her forehead.

In this moment, he was just a man with his woman.

He pressed his face in the haven between her throat and shoulder. And felt...normal.

CHAPTER SIX

"You are very obliging," answered Beauty, "I own I am pleased with your kindness and, when I consider that, your deformity scarce appears."—Beauty and the Beast

"According to Mark Twain kindness is a language the deaf can hear and the blind can see...so is being a jackass."—Gwendolyn Sinclair

"Good morning."

Xavier turned at her greeting. Sunlight poured through the huge picture window of the breakfast room and bathed him in its glow like a halo. She almost snorted at the absurd thought. No angelic being contained the carnal knowledge Xavier had exhibited last night.

Oh damn.

Heat streamed up her neck and rushed to her face. *Hell.* There was no way the intent stare he fixed on her could miss the fiery telltale sign indicating where her thoughts had detoured. And now that the floodgates had opened, she couldn't dam the memories. Her sex softened and a dull ache took up residence at his remembered possession. Oh God, how he'd possessed her. He'd taken control of her body until she hadn't recognized the person she'd become—one focused solely on ecstasy and the man gifting it to her.

She'd twisted under him, begged and cried out for him. A shiver raced over her skin and tingled in her clit. She'd come twice—once on his hands and in his mouth, and then on his cock. She blew out a slow, measured breath even as her heart pounded.

Given his reputation, she hadn't been shocked by his knowledge of a woman's body. The man wore sexuality like most men did a suit or jacket. No, that wasn't accurate. His sensuality couldn't be peeled off as easily as a shirt and tie. It was innate, as much a part of him as his green eyes. So no, his skill hadn't been a surprise. But the tenderness, unselfishness and patience had been. The terms of their bargain dictated she spend seven days at his mercy, for his gratification. Yet he'd placed her pleasure first time and time again.

She stared at his beautiful features and warmth surged into her chest. The thick honey-brown hair drawn into its customary tail only served to enhance the patrician bone structure, the jeweled eyes and carnal curve of his mouth. The reason behind her presence in his home sucked, but maybe, just maybe, they could part friends.

Friends. Her mind scoffed. *As if that's all you want from him.* A woman didn't stop having sex with her fiancé because of *friendship*. Her stomach clenched and she cringed over her inadvertent admission the night before. Under ordinary circumstances—like when not dazed from a mind-blowing orgasm—she wouldn't have confessed the truth about her self-imposed celibacy with Josh. It invited questions...questions she'd rather not answer.

In a world where pumpkins changed into horse-drawn carriages and beasts transformed into princes, Xavier would admire her, his gaze reflecting the love she harbored deep in her heart. But that existence was relegated to Disney films and fairy tales. In the real world, perhaps they could part with her faith in the sensitive, kind, selfless man she'd once known restored. Last night, his passion and gentleness nurtured her dream.

"Good morning, Gwendolyn," he murmured and slid his hands in the front pockets of his gray slacks.

Unease tickled her stomach. Once again, she was Gwendolyn instead of Gwen. Last night, as well as during her bath, he'd called her by the nickname he'd used years ago. With a mental shrug, she shook the disquiet off. Maybe he'd slipped back to formality out of habit.

She moved farther into the room. Cutlery had already been arranged around pristine white plates and steaming platters of food occupied the middle of the table. As she approached the chair Xavier held out for her, she smothered a snicker. Since she'd woken Monday, delicious meals had been prepared for them and the house retained the sparkling clean scent of lemon Pledge, yet she hadn't glimpsed a single employee. Maybe he retained invisible servants like in *Eros and Psyche*.

That was it. *Clash of the Titans* was going to the community center's video library just as soon as she returned home. A week ago she'd compared him to Odysseus and now the star-crossed lovers. No more Greek mythology.

"Thank you." She lowered into the chair and scooted forward. He pulled out the seat next to her at the head of the table and sank into it with a fluid motion she envied and admired. *Hell*. Even the way he sat in a chair was sexy.

The next few moments passed in silence as they selected their breakfast from the platters. Her stomach growled at the mouth-watering scents rising off the variety of sausages, bacon, pancakes and cinnamon rolls. Mortified, she shot a glance at Xavier. But if he heard, he didn't react. Instead he continued to doctor his pancakes with syrup.

The sliver of foreboding made another appearance. His aloof mask and reserved manner wasn't her imagination. She frowned. What had happened between last night and this morning?

"I noticed your stables as I drove up Saturday," she said with deliberate casualness, hoping to draw him into conversation. Anything would be better than the heavy silence. "Do you breed them or are they for pleasure?"

"They're for me."

"Your home is beautiful." She continued even though his short answer and long stare didn't invite chitchat. "I don't remember hearing you talk about this place, though."

He leaned back in his chair and studied her with the same impassive stare. "I bought it a year ago."

Well. Damn.

She dropped her gaze to the plate of food, her fragile hope for a new start with Xavier absconding with her appetite. It didn't require the awesome deduction powers of Sherlock Holmes to figure out the accident and this home in beautiful but remote Great Barrington were connected. A haven with only horses to keep him company. After all, animals responded to kindness, not appearance.

Her heart ached for him in spite of his distant behavior. This man should be at the heart of parties, surrounded by people hanging on his every word. Not relegated to the outskirts, tolerated when he couldn't be avoided. As if he were to blame for a tragedy beyond his control. Reviled for a mark that displayed his strength and iron will in the face of suffering others would have broken under.

"What are you thinking?"

The low, quiet voice sounded so much like the tone he'd used with her the night before, it startled her into answering honestly.

"You're beautiful," she blurted.

His face hardened, but not before a spasm of pain disappeared under the forbidding mask. Eyes that had been cold a moment ago were now glacial—two jagged pieces of ice to pierce her soul.

"The nature of our bargain eliminates the need for empty flattery. Especially when we both know it's a lie." He lashed out, leaving bleeding lacerations. "But if it makes you feel better to indulge in fantasy, come sit on this side of me." He patted the table with his right hand. "The view's better."

Raw bitterness and anger seethed beneath the callous remark. The resentment and fury concealed behind the reserve he showed the world festered in places so deep, Gwendolyn couldn't reach them. Grief tore through her as if someone had died. And she supposed someone had—the loving, compassionate man who no longer existed. In his place sat this embittered stranger, the scars he carried on his soul more devastating than the one marring the left side of his face.

"Is this how it's going to be between us for the next five days?" she asked quietly. "Where we can't even talk?"

"I thought I made it clear what you're here for, Gwendolyn. And it's not talking."

She shoved back her chair and rose to her feet. Anger and an overwhelming sorrow encompassed her. She'd believed Xavier had chosen to live. That had been a façade too. He existed with rage and hostility as faithful companions, leaving room for no one else.

"That's right," she said. Silently, she cursed the tears stinging her eyes and tilted her chin up as if the gesture could prevent them from spilling. "As you take such great delight in reminding me. Why don't you leave money on the nightstand? That would show me. Consider it a tip." Her voice thickened and she hated herself for the sign of weakness. Hated him. "Or better yet, just subtract it off the top of the money I'm spreading my legs for."

"Stop it!"

The harsh order didn't penetrate the hurt—the blinding hurt and fury that ate a hole in her heart. *Stupid!* God, she was so stupid for believing one night of sex could soften his feelings toward her. Could soften him.

"Stop what? I'm just repeating what you've been drilling into my head since I agreed to this damn deal."

"Gwendolyn," he growled over the scrape of his chair as he shot to his feet.

"Just—" Her voice broke. She whirled and stalked toward the door. Dammit, she refused to let him see one fucking tear fall. Not. One. "Just go to hell."

CHAPTER SEVEN

"Among mankind," says Beauty, "there are many that deserve that name more than you, and I prefer you, just as you are, to those who under a human form hide a treacherous, corrupt and ungrateful heart."—Beauty and the Beast

"Beauty is only skin deep... That's some bullshit."—Xavier St. James

Why don't you leave money on the nightstand? That would show me. Consider it a tip. Or better yet, just subtract it off the top of the money I'm spreading my legs for.

You're beautiful.

Gwendolyn's words from the morning echoed in his head like a CD stuck on replay. He gazed out the dark dining room window, his reflection like a condemning finger pointing back at him. His fists tightened at his sides. God, her words had hurt. Both her accusation about him treating her like a whore and the lie about his beauty. It was a toss-up which stabbed deepest.

Xavier closed his eyes and for once it wasn't to shut out the sight of his ruined face.

He could no longer bear the sight of the entire man. When had he become such a cowardly bastard?

His gutlessness shamed him. He'd considered himself strong. Losing his brother had devastated him, but he'd endured. Then years later, the sudden loss of his father followed by Evelyn's abandonment had nearly brought him to his knees. He almost hadn't recovered from the blow of losing the man he'd admired above all others. But he *had* survived. Then Evelyn had walked out.

Her desertion had almost broken him. The signs had been there—her refusal to look him directly in the face, her reluctance to be seen with him in public because of the stares. Yet he still hadn't expected her betrayal because he'd believed they were in love. Or that he'd loved her.

No, Evelyn hadn't broken him. But she'd damn well shattered something inside him.

When she left, she'd broken the last tenuous link to his life before the accident. The charmed years filled with family, friends and joy were irrevocably gone, leaving him no clue how to deal with the new existence fate had dealt him. His family would never be whole again. Those he'd called friends had turned their backs on him and he was alone. So fucking alone.

Enter Gwendolyn.

He sucked in a breath and opened his eyes. Instead of his likeness, he viewed flashes of the previous night in the darkened glass. His stomach tightened with arousal and his cock swelled at the remembered slick grip of her pussy. Of her skin pressed to his. Of her arms wrapped around him, holding him close. Locked in her embrace, the loneliness had vanished.

And its absence had scared the shit out of him.

After she'd drifted to sleep, he'd curled up behind her and dreams—impossible dreams—had stirred in his heart. Love. A woman who wanted him in spite of his imperfections. A family of his own. Fear had spurred him out of the warm bed and tangled sheets. As he'd jerked on his clothes, he shut down the faint, burgeoning longings of love, acceptance and happiness. And he'd refused himself one last look at the sleeping woman.

There were no happily ever afters for him.

He would be a fool to become attached to Gwendolyn. The only reason she slumbered in his bed was due to fucking blackmail. If not for the community center, he would be as alone as he'd been for the past year.

He and Gwendolyn had a business contract. Nothing more.

But his determination to set their relationship back on the agreed-upon terms didn't excuse the hurt in her eyes this morning. Hurt he'd inflicted. They could make love—*no, damn it, have sex*. They could *have sex* and maintain the distance needed to walk away without wounding each other.

Hell, he snorted, turning away from the window. He should know. Before Evelyn he'd been the prince of casual affairs. He'd expected the women he fucked not to become emotionally entangled *and* to remain friends after their time together ended.

That shoe throbbed like hell since it had become wedged on the other foot.

He scanned the dining room and then the empty doorway. A quick inspection of his watch revealed the hour. Seven-thirty. Gwendolyn should've been downstairs for dinner thirty minutes ago. Worry pinched his chest. He frowned and hesitated just a moment before striding from the room. He crossed the foyer and loped up the stairs, unease a steadily tightening knot in his stomach.

What if she'd had a relapse? Damn. He should have granted her another day to recover before demanding sex. He scowled, rushing down the hallway. He'd assumed her absence today had been due to their argument at breakfast, but maybe she'd been sick. Maybe the fever had flared up and she'd been too angry to call for him.

Xavier swung open the door to her bedroom. His grip on the knob prevented the wood from smacking the wall behind it. Finding the bed empty, he skimmed the rest of the room until he located Gwendolyn, the picture of perfect health, perched on the wide window seat, a book in her lap and gaping at him as if he'd flown over the cuckoo's nest.

Even as anger kindled in his gut and replaced the concern, his body tensed, heated. Hardened. The smooth skin on her shoulders and toned arms glowed in the soft light of the bedroom lamps. Bare feet peeked out from under her thigh, the innocence of her position incongruous with the natural sensuality she exuded like a perfumed scent. Maybe that explained his powerful reaction. The animal in him detected some unique pheromone she emanated and went wild with a whiff of it.

He shoved the door shut and her eyes widened at the loud crack of wood meeting wood.

"What are you doing?" She laid the book aside and rose to her feet, the motion slow as if she sensed his intention to pounce.

"Why weren't you at dinner?"

She straightened her shoulders, her body as rigid as the stern set of her full lips. "I didn't see the point of going through formalities. As you mentioned earlier, there's no need for it."

Anger flared bright and hot before chilling to an icy resolve. And the bullshit he'd repeated to himself since leaving her bed last night, the same he'd finished reciting in the dining room, sounded just like that—bullshit.

If he'd wanted an automaton, he would've continued fucking escorts instead of his hand. But not possessing the same passionate, uninhibited woman he'd been balls-deep in the previous evening? Not an option. He didn't just want her body. He wanted her fire, her unselfishness.

He wanted Gwen. Nothing less than all of her would do.

From the moment she'd sought him out for help, he'd demanded everything from her—her body, her submission, her trust—and had offered nothing in return.

His turn to put up or shut up had arrived.

He fisted the front of his shirt. A pit yawned wide in his stomach and his heart plummeted toward the dizzying, black depth. The last woman to glimpse what lay under his shirt and pants had been so disgusted she'd abandoned him. Fear coated his mouth, his nostrils. All he tasted and smelled were ash and smoke. For a brief moment, he considered whirling around and walking out. Shame flayed him and the stranglehold he had on his shirt tightened. The idea of baring the map of scars disfiguring his body scared him shitless.

But if he desired her trust, he had to battle his fears, emerge from behind the false protection of pride and seize this last chance to make amends with her. A last chance to show Gwen her fire, touch and uninhibited response meant more than his pride. *She* meant more.

He inhaled. Exhaled.

And yanked the shirttails from the band of his pants.

The unyielding line of her mouth softened, her lips parted and, as he freed the small buttons from their corresponding holes, her sharp intake of breath reached across the room.

Damn, he loved witnessing the evidence of his effect on her. Hours on a shrink's couch couldn't begin to heal his battered, broken spirit like one soft, sensuous gasp from this beautiful, giving woman.

"What are you doing?" she demanded, the small tremble in her voice undermining the show of bravado.

He gripped the sides of the black material, his fingers tightening for a long instant before he shrugged it off his shoulders.

"Getting undressed." He tugged his belt buckle open. "Now get naked."

Good God, the man is ripped.

* * * * *

Golden skin stretched taut over lean, firm muscles that tugged and bunched in a mouthwatering display as he shed the shirt and let it fall in a pool of black material behind him. The anger she'd nursed all day melted under the heat of desire as soon as the first slice of skin appeared. Her heart thumped hard and then drummed in a fast, deafening tattoo. Blood pounded in her veins and filled the flesh between her legs. Dew gathered on the swollen lips and her pussy clenched when he pulled his belt buckle free.

Then his order to "get naked" doused her in the face like an arctic spray of water. "What?" she asked and frowned. "Wait." Was he kidding? She shook her head.

"No."

Xavier arched an eyebrow but didn't stop sliding the belt from his pant loops. "Take your clothes off, Gwendolyn."

"No." She shook her head more vehemently. "Not like this."

"Like what?" The rasp of his zipper lowering was a discordant note in the quiet room.

"In anger."

He paused and his eyebrows arched high, his lips slightly parted. "Anger?" he repeated and resumed toeing off his shoes. "I'm hard, baby. Not angry."

He shoved his pants and underwear down his hips and thighs, then stepped free of the clothes at his feet. Xavier straightened to his full height, robbing her of breath and speech with the full impact of his naked body.

Last night before removing his shirt and pants, he'd extinguished the room's lamp. As she'd caressed him, her fingers had skimmed the raised edges that crisscrossed his chest, abdomen and back. His wish for darkness had fully dawned on her then. His body had not been left unscathed by the accident. And he feared her reaction. But now—standing before her in the lit room, bare to her gaze—tears stung her eyes.

He is beautiful.

Honeyed skin melted over a body Hephaestus could've forged

himself. Toned, strong muscles contracted and relaxed with each movement like an orchestra performing in perfect harmony. She lowered her inspection. God, the man even had sexy feet! Her wry amusement converted to a hot, startling rush of lust as she lifted her gaze to the long, ponderous weight of his cock. It hung down his thigh, the wide flared head the size of a plum. As if all the air had been vacuumed from the room, Gwendolyn experienced a moment of lightheadedness. How in the hell had he fit all of that inside her?

But he had. He'd filled every inch of her pussy. His cock had branded her, stamped its ownership. A disquieting sense of foreboding curdled in her belly. For years no man, not even Joshua, had compared to Xavier's sensual vitality and beauty. And he hadn't even touched her then. But now…now that she'd been caressed and stroked by him, no one would fill her—complete her—as he had last night.

Under her close scrutiny, the thick shaft lengthened another impossible increment. Her heart thudded in a dull, heavy rhythm. Did anticipation, arousal or fear pound through her veins and echo in her clit? Maybe all three.

"I'm still waiting, Gwendolyn." His husky tone transformed the order into an invitation—an invitation to revisit the exquisite pleasure of the previous evening. She'd lost herself in passion so overwhelming, she'd been almost bruised by it, as if ecstasy had been the waves and she'd been the shore they'd crashed upon.

Trembling, she slid the straps of her tank from her shoulders and pushed the top down her torso, hips and legs, taking the cotton bottoms with it. As she straightened, she tried to convince herself she complied because their deal left her no choice. If he released her from this devil's bargain, she would snatch up her clothes, leave the room and house and never see him again. But even if she could persuade herself she would've walked away, the cream coating the sensitive flesh between her thighs branded her a liar with a huge "L" stamped on her chest.

She drank in his battle-scarred beauty and confessed in the most secret part of her soul she was glad he didn't offer her the choice to leave. Because then she would have to admit the community center and the people there didn't keep her in the bedroom. As much as she loved them, Xavier glued her feet to the floor. Desire did.

Love did.

As angry and hurt as she'd been today, neither response could override the potent emotion she'd harbored for years—an emotion so powerful she'd driven hours with a raging fever just to spend a few days with him. Even without the money for the center hanging over her head like Damocles' sword, she would have agreed to this week with him.

That damn money.

She dropped her gaze. Hindsight had the vision of an eagle. If she had never approached him about the grant, he wouldn't have the money to pitch in her face every time she dared rub too close to the festering wound in his heart and soul. The irony didn't escape her. He would never have allowed her in his home, in his bed, without the deal. Xavier with his scarred face, body and soul, wouldn't have believed she wanted him—loved him.

So should she accept the money and stay with him, steal what time they had left? Or tell him to hell with the money, she wanted to remain because of her feelings for him, and be evicted so fast her ass would leave skid marks on his pristine wood floors?

Either choice resulted in being thrown out of his house. But only one granted her a precious slice of time in his bed, his arms…his life.

"Get on the bed."

The quiet command drew her attention back to him. Xavier had moved to the small dresser flanking the bed. Though his eyes tracked her slow progress, he pulled open the top drawer, dipped his hand inside and pulled an object free. Gwendolyn flicked a glance at his fist and pulled up short. Shock, apprehension and a sliver of…excitement sliced through her.

Thin, shiny black strips dangled from his closed hand.

Ties. Recognition slapped her and she jerked her inspection to his face. The stark mask of lust snatched the breath from her throat. Skin stretched tight over his cheekbones. Nostrils flared slightly as if to catch the perfume of her arousal. His green eyes glittered and the sensual fullness of his lips flattened into a straight, hard line. As if his hungry stare were the match and her arousal the accelerant, heat whooshed through her veins like a flash fire, setting her breasts and sex aflame. A small moan escaped her throat and his gaze narrowed, sharpened.

What was happening to her? She'd never gone for extreme sex games or BDSM. Granted, until last night, her sex life had been very tame and sedate—nice, but not the screaming, cataclysmic experience Xavier had supplied her. But still she didn't like being tied up, bent over or spanked...did she?

"On the bed, Gwendolyn," he repeated and the low, rough timbre stroked over her skin like a calloused hand—gentle, yet hard enough to leave tingles behind. Like a drunken woman, she stumbled the last few feet until her thighs bumped the edge of the mattress. She raised a bent knee and rested it on the covers. On the other side of the bed, Xavier mimicked her movements. In seconds they both knelt, facing each other like an erotic game of chicken. "Give me your hands."

Disobedience wasn't an option. Yes, she was in the dark regarding his intentions, but she wanted whatever he could give her. God, did she want it. Wanted *him*. She extended her arms, fists down, and Xavier engulfed her hand within his larger one. He turned the fist over, opened it and grazed the sensitive skin of her palm with his fingertips. The small stroke reverberated in her clit and she bit back a gasp.

He drew a tiny circle and, this time, she didn't contain the moan. Or the groan. And when he lifted his finger to his mouth, sucked on the tip and traced a damp line from her wrist to the base of her thumb, she trembled and squeezed her thighs against the fluttering in her pussy. Such a benign caress and yet it echoed between her legs as if he'd traced the crease of her pulsing sex.

With her skin still tingling from his touch, Xavier laid the leather ties across her open palm. She stared down at the slender black strips, lost.

She frowned, glanced up at him. "Xavier?"

Her bewilderment increased when he released her and presented his loosely closed fists as if he wanted her to... No, he couldn't intend...

But one glance at his hooded eyes and the grim set of his mouth confirmed her suspicions. The ties weren't meant for her...but for him.

She clutched the slim, leather straps and their inconsequential weight was incongruous when compared to their significance. This man who prized control and trusted no one had handed her a tiny measure of both.

She closed her eyes and hope jimmied open her heart and the tiniest degree slipped through once again. With a sigh that sounded more like a sob, she lifted her lashes and fastened the ends of the ties around his thick wrists.

Silent, his intense, bright stare fixed on her, Xavier reclined on the bed and stretched his arms above his head. The sinew and tendons were delineated beneath his golden skin like a powerful, deadly panther at rest yet ready to spring at the slightest threat…or sight of prey.

With a slight shift, she knelt at his side, her knees brushing the soft patch of fur beneath his arm. Controlling the tremble in her fingers as she tied the leather strips to the bedpost proved impossible. The resulting knot wouldn't present a challenge should he decide to break free, but it was all her virgin bondage skills could manage.

Awkward and more than a little embarrassed, she straddled his torso. She transferred her weight, preparing to move to the other side of his body in order to reach the last binding. Even as she lifted her leg, his small inhalation stopped her. She dropped her gaze and *good God*. Her core contracted and a wave of desire almost propelled her down to his chest.

Long, dark lashes concealed his gemlike stare. His thin, aristocratic nostrils flared and his chest rose to press her opened sex as he deeply drew in her scent. His full, sensual lips parted as if he tasted the aroma signaling her arousal. The unguarded, pure delight softened his features and lanced her heart. Outside this bedroom, he would never reveal such an uninhibited, honest delight. He would consider the reaction a vulnerability, a weakness. But here in this bed, he admitted a glimpse into the hedonistic animal that enjoyed pleasure and reciprocating it.

He raised his eyelids and his intent inspection ignited a fire in her only he could extinguish. An image of her rubbing over his body in a long, sinuous caress like a cat in heat flashed across her mind's eye. She longed to discard every perception of sex she'd ever harbored and redefine it with him. Let him show her what desire, touching and ecstasy entailed.

If this man was the poisonous fruit, she would gladly gorge on it and dive into Death's embrace. He would so be worth the sin and fall.

Her pulse accelerated as she swung her leg over his body and completed binding him to the bed. The deed done, she didn't resist the impulse to trail a caress down the corded muscle under his arm. She leaned back on her haunches and beheld Xavier bound, stretched and contained.

Like a harnessed tornado—dangerous and wildly exciting.

His wide chest rose and fell in deep, measured breaths, causing his ridged abdomen to stand out in stark relief. She longed to savor every intriguing crest and dip of his rib cage. Travel to the shallow indentation of his navel. Curl her fingers through the wiry, russet thatch of hair surrounding the thick, long column of flesh flexing next to his muscled thigh. Smooth her cheek over his cock and inhale the musky, sexy, spicy scent belonging solely to him.

"Why?" she whispered, the reason flickering like a tiny spark of longing against the encompassing darkness of fear. She wanted him to speak the words and fan the flame sputtering in the face of her doubt.

"I've taken from you, Gwen," he murmured. "Take from me. All I have to give." Though his hands were restrained, his hot stare stroked her as if they were unbound, free to stir her desire to a fever pitch.

All that I have to give. Not the declaration her heart desired to hear, but more than she had this morning. And for now, with his trusting her with his body and satisfaction, the offer was enough.

The inside of her thigh slid over his abdomen as she reclaimed her position astride his upper body. A hum of delight caught her by surprise—she hadn't meant to release it. But as she stroked her palms over the firm plane of his chest and the small, hard pebbles of his dark-brown nipples grazed her skin, shivers coursed up her arms to her breasts, down her stomach and settled in her clit like a low-level buzz of electricity.

His beauty awed her.

She formed a bracket with her thumbs on either side of the thin patch of skin that throbbed in the dip of his throat. His life's blood pounded under her touch and the primal rhythm surged through her, connecting them. Gently, she cupped his face and lowered her forehead to his until their breath mingled, mated. His soft sigh reached her seconds before he tipped his chin upward and claimed her mouth.

How did he manage to wrest control from her when he was the one bound? He pierced her lips with his tongue and licked the roof of her mouth, inviting her to join the sensuous ballet.

She emitted a groan. He did have complete domination.

His wild, wind-and-rain taste overwhelmed her. He nipped her bottom lip and the slight sting arrowed straight to her pussy. Her quick puffs of breath filled his mouth as she ground the pad of her sex against his abdomen, seeking relief from the swelling ache. She cradled his scalp, tipped his chin up farther with her thumbs and reclaimed control. She ate him up like rich, sweet chocolate. She was greedy, gluttonous, returning to his mouth time and time again for more of his lush, decadent flavor.

Hot blasts of air heated her lips as Xavier panted beneath her. He lifted his head from the pillow, the tendons in his neck stretching against his dusky skin as he reached for her, silently demanding more. She tore her mouth from his, planted her palms on either side of his head and stared down at him. His chest rose and fell in labored breaths. His eyes gleamed from under lowered lids, beckoning her to feast on him again. Damn, did she want to concede to the invitation. But first...

She straightened and once again cupped his jaw. His lashes fluttered, but didn't lower. When she slid her fingers over his temples and under his head to the bound tail of hair, his eyes widened and a flicker of panic flared in their emerald depths. A fist squeezed her heart at the spark of anxiety, but she steeled her resolve and untied the band imprisoning his hair. His powerful body tensed beneath her thighs and his features—lax with contentment a moment ago—slowly stiffened as if bracing for a blow.

She massaged his scalp to reassure him he was safe with her and spread the thick strands over the white pillowcase like a dark cape. So beautiful. She sighed and gripped a handful of the heavy, mahogany mane, lifted it to her nose and luxuriated in the surprisingly soft silk and clean, fresh scent.

"Don't," he objected hoarsely.

Her heart twisted at the desperate fear roughening his voice, but she forged on. "Shhh..." she whispered soothingly and let the long hair sift through her fingers as it drifted back down to the pillow. He studied her as she leaned over him, his gaze intent. The stark planes of his face remained set in rigid lines, reminding her of the contained stranger she'd confronted a week ago...and encountered that morning.

73

But the man from earlier wouldn't have allowed her to bind him to the bed, submitting his body and control. Leaving himself vulnerable. She'd walk away from this bed, this house, before betraying the courage it had taken him to stretch out before her naked in body and soul.

She took his mouth in a tender kiss. At first his lips remained unyielding, but she continued her sensual assault, nuzzling, nipping, until with a soft moan he gave in and his lips parted underneath hers.

"I think I could kiss you forever." The admission escaped her before she could snatch it back. Heat, unrelated to passion, warmed her cheeks.

"And yet you stopped."

Her heart missed a beat and then raced to catch up.

"I'm not even close to stopping." She trailed a damp path down his chin and over the line of his jaw. Her lips bumped the ridge of flesh marring his chin and his body stiffened. She brushed a caress over the mark and ignored his low hiss of breath.

It would've been so easy to acquiesce to his "hands off" body language and move on to his neck or shoulders.

But not tonight. Not when she could show him how beautiful she found him—scars and all—without him being able to walk away or shut her down.

The length of the scar from chin to hairline received her devotion. Without words, she declared his loveliness. Hot blasts of breath seared her cheek as his hoarse rasps echoed in the silent room. The tendons in his neck stood out in sharp relief as if any moment he might throw his head back against the pillow to evade her touch.

Yet he remained still as a statue except for his heaving chest.

Again her heart wrenched at the sign of his obvious agitation, but she didn't stop.

When she moved on to his chest and abdomen, she began the homage all over again.

By the time she returned to his mouth, his muscles had loosened, the austere lines of his face had softened and a faint flush painted his high cheekbones. Instead of rough inhalations, low pants rushed in and out of his parted lips. She studied his sensual features and met his stare, glowing with desire and something so raw, so wild she couldn't name it...was afraid to label it.

"I want your mouth on me," she murmured and nuzzled the curve of his ear, empowered, emboldened by his restraint and her passion. "Will you make me come, Xavier? Make me cry out your name? Make me beg even though I'm the one in control? Can you do that?"

His gaze widened in surprise before narrowing. How he could resemble a predator while tied and imprisoned baffled her. Even more confounding was how she could shake like the prey caught in his sights.

"Slide up for me, Gwen." His husky command shivered down her spine and caused more liquid to dampen her thighs. Unable to prevent the motion, she circled her hips over his chest, the movement exerting direct pressure on her clit. The slow grind inflamed and satisfied the pounding ache and she groaned. "Come on, baby. I can't give you what you need unless you move. As much as I love seeing you explode, I'd rather have your sweet cream in my mouth than decorating my body."

The words and underlying hint of strained laughter urged her forward. In moments, she had one knee beside his head and the other on the outside of his cuffed arm.

"Grab the headboard."

She glanced down her torso and bit back a pained cry. Though searing desire coursed through her and weighed her eyelids, she forced her eyes to remain open. She didn't want to miss the erotic vision of Xavier staring up at her from between her spread thighs, his full lips only a breath away from grazing her aching flesh. Seconds from dipping his talented tongue into her core and driving her to heights only he could carry her.

She whimpered.

Then lifted a knee and whipped around. "Gwen?"

She ignored his raspy question and planted her palms next to his narrow hips. His long, steely erection lay against his stomach like an intimidating length of thick pipe topped by a flushed, smooth cap. A drop of precum beaded at the slit as if welling just from her captivated gaze. Jesus, he was beautiful. Like Michelangelo's *David*. Sculpted, virile and perfect.

"Gwen," he repeated. "This isn't for me, baby. You don't have to do this."

"I know," she responded, already reaching for his cock. Just thinking about what his flesh could do inside her pussy made her clit pound and her empty core spasm. "This *is* for me."

To have him fill her mouth, to discover if the same wind-and-rain taste of his kiss would transfer to his cock... Yes, this was all for her.

She leaned down and engulfed the bulbous head. Immediately his untamed flavor detonated on her tongue and she moaned with excitement. She squeezed his flesh, stroking her fist up the hard shaft until her fingers bumped her stretched lips. Another spurt of his seed pulsed from the narrow opening and she lapped at his salty essence. God, it was just so *good*.

"Dammit, Gwen." Xavier's hungry growl penetrated her lust. "Give me your pussy.

Now."

She released his cock with a small *pop* and stared, bemused, at the wet head. She'd been so engrossed in finally having him in her mouth, she'd forgotten about her original request. With a small shake of her head, she lowered her lips to his erection and her pussy to his mouth.

"Oh God, Xavier!" She flung her head back as the scream ripped from her throat. He thrust his tongue past her cream-coated folds to the clenching tunnel beyond. "Please, no...yes," she sobbed as he stabbed deep. "Yes."

He licked her, consumed her. His teeth latched on to one swollen lip and he sucked, flicked and laved it before moving to the other. Though he was tied to the bed, he mastered her as if he were unbound, gripping her hips and guiding this seductive meltdown. His mouth held her captive and all she could do was follow his lead.

"Fuck my mouth, baby," he ordered, his hot breath an added caress to her sensitive flesh. "Ride it like my cock."

His cock. Damn. She'd forgotten all about pleasuring him while his tongue tormented her pussy. She tightened her grip on his stalk and stroked down to the wide, flared base, then returned up and over the head. On the return trip down, precum lubricated the path until her fist glided back and forth, back and forth in a relentless rhythm.

"That's it," Xavier encouraged on the tail of a harsh groan. "Squeeze it tight, baby."

Gwen imagined if his hands were free, he would've swatted her ass. How she conjured that particular picture—or why her core spasmed in excitement—she couldn't explain. Except... Until Xavier, maybe she hadn't known what she desired from a lover. Not until he'd shown her.

She knelt over her lover, his lips and tongue buried in her pussy while she fisted his cock.

"God, you're sweet, Gwen," he murmured over her clit before sipping at the engorged, aching button.

"Xavier." She gasped and couldn't have prevented the buck of her hips if she'd been threatened to hold still. "Please. Again. Harder. Suck me harder."

As if to torment her, he flicked her flesh, the touch light and teasing and nowhere close to the pressure she needed.

"Don't tease me," she demanded. Two could play at torment. She suckled his gleaming cock head. She bathed the tip with long, slow licks and alternated with strong, hard pulls.

"Fuck," he growled and then ended her suffering. Giving her no quarter, he clamped down on her clit and drew hard. He sucked, nipped and encircled her flesh. Heat gathered in the nub and eddied in ever-increasing pools of pleasure. As he feasted on her pussy, she rode his face, the wet sounds of his mouth adding to the surreal sensuality. Once more she let go of his cock to immerse herself in the wild, carnal passion.

It crashed on her. The orgasm didn't swell or creep, but broke over her like a sonic blast, its waves echoing against her skin in one powerful surge after another. She screamed with the ecstasy of release. Trembled over him. Quaked over him. Seizures gripped her in their seismic hold and racked her body.

She plummeted back to the realm of the living and pitched forward to rest her cheek on his jutting hip bone. Her eyes opened and the broad base of his cock surrounded by dark, springy hair greeted her. Her quick blasts of air stirred the curls and his musky, tantalizing scent of sweat, skin and sex caused her to shudder.

"Gwen." She shifted, his breath an almost unbearable caress on her vulnerable flesh. "Gwen," he repeated. She roused at the urgent knot in his strained voice and slid off his chest. She curled up next to him, her knees pressed into the sides of his torso. "Baby, I need you." From her vantage point, his strong throat worked as he swallowed. "I'm going to go crazy if I'm not inside you. Fuck me, sweetheart," he whispered.

The plea moved her like nothing else could have. She scrambled to her knees and, in spite of her sated lethargy, slid off the bed and jerked open the drawer in the bedside table. Quickly, she ripped the top of the foil packet and removed the condom before straddling his hips and sheathing his erection in the latex.

With one hand, she positioned his cock so the head prodded her slit, the palm of her other hand pressed against his abdomen. Muscles flexed and tightened beneath her touch as if in preparation for thrusting between her folds and being gloved in her sex.

She glanced past his chest to his tightly drawn features. The bright, jeweled gaze stared back at her, burning like the heart of the hottest fire. Every muscle in his body was drawn as tight as a bow. If she freed his hands in this moment, he would no doubt spring up and take her down like felled prey.

Slowly she rubbed the cock head through her crease, wetting the wide cap in her silky folds. The broad tip bumped against her clit, skimming the sensitive bundle of nerves, and she inhaled sharply. *Oh yes.* She hummed. *Just once…more.* She whimpered. And did it again.

"Don't tease me," he said, flinging her earlier demand at her, his arms straining against the restraints. "I'm at the breaking point, baby. Put me inside."

She shivered. Yes, she delighted in the brush of his cock on her clit, but she craved to be filled by him as much as he needed it. She nudged the cock head between her folds and sank down.

She gasped at the tight fit. Last night he'd been so large at first she'd been afraid they wouldn't fit. He'd reached for her once more as night tipped over into morning, taking her again, so she should be used to his size, but the pressure now was heavy and delicious. God, it hurt so—she sank down another inch—*good.* She glanced down at the thick, veined stalk yet left to take and wanted to groan in anticipation…and a tad bit of trepidation. There was so much of him.

"Look at me, Gwen." His husky voice drew her attention from the intimidating length of his cock to his face. The hard, taut features belied his gentle tone. "It's the position that makes taking me a little more difficult. But you can do it, baby. You can take my cock inside you. I want to be balls-deep, sweetheart. I don't want an inch of my cock left untouched by the sweetest pussy I've ever fucked. Come on, Gwen. Take it." His timbre deepened as he studied her from under his gleaming, sensual gaze. "Take me."

Surely the serpent's tempting of Eve couldn't have been more seductive than his invitation. And the result was the same. She gripped his erection and pressed down. The wide length burrowed into her spasming pussy. She moaned, flexed her hips. And another couple inches disappeared into her flesh.

So full. She held still and allowed her body to accustom itself to the penetration. With both palms planted on his ribs, she raised her hips off his cock and slowly—so slowly—descended, taking more of him. Delight rippled through her core and she gasped. Eagerly, she duplicated the motion and hissed out a breath as her existence narrowed to include only desire and Xavier. She slid up his shaft until just the rounded peak of the head remained inside her clutching entrance. And then she sank back down, engulfing more of his length than she'd claimed on the previous trip. Each slow stroke drew a cry from her so the quiet room was punctuated by her whimpers and the wet suction of her pussy fucking his cock. It was the sweetest music she'd ever heard.

"Dammit, Gwen," Xavier growled, his back bowing. "Get down on my dick." His hips jerked hard and in spite of the leverage her hands provided, more of his rigid column penetrated her tight sheath. "Now, Gwen."

"So," she groaned, squeezing her muscles as she lifted off him, "impatient."

She glanced down. She'd taken a little over half of him, yet the thickest, fattest part of his shaft still remained to be conquered. Sweat poured in rivulets down the vee between her breasts and she shuddered at the pressure between her thighs. God, she was stretched, filled, but she wanted all of him. The slow ride she'd been enjoying wasn't enough anymore. She hungered to have every inch of him embedded deep so next week, when he was gone from her life again, she would still feel him.

Inhaling, she flattened her palms on his chest, tightened her thighs and glanced up at him. "Help me," she whispered.

His eyes glittered and, as one, he thrust upward as she surged down.

A hoarse cry erupted from her joined by his raw groan. Oh God. Oh. God. Possessed...she was possessed. As her muscles quivered madly around his cock, as he occupied her pussy, leaving nothing untouched, she became a new creature, one forever imprinted with Xavier's mark. She'd never be free of him.

"Shhh..." he soothed as his big body shuddered beneath her. Only then did she realize soft whimpers were coming from her throat. "It's okay, baby. I can feel you surrounding me. You're so sweet, so—" His voice broke and a strong tremor shuddered over him. The vibration thrummed through her stretched pussy. "Fuck me, baby. Take me away from here, Gwen. Take me to heaven."

She swallowed. His words—the plea beneath—penetrated her heart as surely as his erection pierced her flesh. Trembling, she rolled and pitched her hips, allowing the intoxicating excitement to consume her. On every downward stroke, his cock head rubbed a place high inside her she hadn't known existed. Her clit hummed as if electricity had a direct route to the nerve-packed bundle.

"Yes, baby," he moaned, meeting each thrust with one of his own. "Harder. Damn, you're so good."

His words spurred her on until she rode him with abandon. Her walls grasped at his dick with each withdrawal as if reluctant to release him, eagerly sucking him back in her depths on the plunge downward.

She wanted the wild ride to continue forever, but as the orgasm neared, tingling at the base of her spine, pressing against her clit, holding on didn't remain an option. So she welcomed the explosion. Hurled herself into the fiery cataclysm, unknowing if she would be reborn or incinerate in the flames.

Through the roar in her head and the frantic hammering of her heart, Xavier joined her. And even as sweet oblivion opened its arms to her, she wasn't alone in the darkness. Never alone.

CHAPTER EIGHT

"I will send you to your father, you shall remain with him, and poor Beast will die with grief."

—*Beauty and the Beast*

"Dying is easy. It's living that's a kick in the ass."—*Xavier St. James*

The September sun painted the world with a gilded brush. The green pastures were vibrant, jeweled acres, the brick red of the stables glowed crimson and the sable coats of the frolicking horses gleamed with health and vitality. Though fall had barely arrived, the morning air contained a small nip even though winter's grasp still remained several weeks away.

A perfect morning.

Gwendolyn sighed and tilted her head back, and the sun's rays teased her face with their warmth. Yes, a perfect morning...if she wasn't out here at the corral, avoiding. Well maybe *hiding* would be a better word. They both amounted to the same thing, but avoidance didn't seem as cowardly.

She flicked a glance over her shoulder toward the house. It stood like an elegant, imposing sentinel against the clear crystal-blue sky. An apt description for its master. Urbane. Commanding. Guardian of this haven he'd created for himself in the beautiful Berkshires mountains. A refuge far from the shallow glitz and glamour of

Boston society. A refuge where he probably allowed no one entrance.

Except her.

"Oh damn," she mumbled, turned and rested her forehead on top of her folded arms. The wooden railing of the corral bit the underside of her arm through the thin jacket she'd donned in deference to the cool morning air. She ignored the slight discomfort, too preoccupied by the much sharper pain brutal honesty often caused.

She was so screwed.

A rough chuckle escaped her throat and it carried the edge of despair. Since Xavier had delivered his bargain, she'd used martyrdom for the community center as justification for agreeing to his terms. Though still beaten up by recriminations over Joshua's death, her need to help the community center outweighed her guilt. Being the sacrificial lamb had enabled her to accept the offer.

But after last night, she could no longer sail along the banks of "De Nile". The community center had been a convenient excuse, and the unvarnished, stark truth was she'd arrived at his home and agreed to be mistress to the beast because she loved him. To grab her one chance at being with him. For years she'd dreamed of being possessed by him. She'd hungered to know the joy of being in his arms, of holding his body close while they exploded in an ecstasy she'd instinctively known only he could bring her.

She'd experienced both. And the intimacy, the bliss had far exceeded her fantasies. So what could she do? Where did she go from here? How could she drive away at the end of these seven days and pretend she wasn't leaving her heart behind as well?

After making love the night before, she'd released Xavier from the ties and he had enfolded her in his arms, held her close and pressed his lips to her temple. The tenderness of his embrace had shattered something inside her. Yes, she'd betrayed Joshua for years by loving his brother and not mustering the courage to confess the truth. But how much longer could she flay herself over a mistake? Especially when the beauty she'd experienced with Xavier edged out the grief, purified her of the shame. Love had stripped away fear, guilt and pride. This man who had submitted his strength and vulnerability to her deserved no less than her honesty.

She'd whispered his name, prepared to admit everything—her love for him, her role in Joshua's death—but Xavier had covered her mouth with his and made love to her again. And when sunlight had spilled across her bed the next morning, she'd been alone.

And now doubt and her ol' albatross—fear—had crept back in.

She propped her chin on her arms and closed her eyes. Last night she'd been ready to lay her sins out before him. But hours later, the thought of facing his derision or worse—his disgust—terrified her. Twisted her stomach into knots so tight, it might be permanently kinked.

"Good morning."

She straightened and whirled at the husky greeting. Surprise and delight bubbled in her chest. Every time she met his green eyes she was transported back to the time when she was a shy teen, eager and happy to just grab a glimpse of him. Some things didn't change. He still wielded the power to incite pandemonium in her pulse.

As usual, his rich golden-brown hair was restrained, but the intent stare—while holding none of the heat in their depths from the night before—didn't contain the aloof frost from the previous morning.

Cautious. His quiet regard was cautious. As if he was unsure of her frame of mind in the revealing light of a new morning. She snorted silently. Join the club.

"Hey," she returned and cleared her throat. And dropped her gaze. And rubbed her palms down the front of her pants. Silly. After all they'd shared, she was like a girl in front of her high school crush.

"Have you ever ridden before?"

She stared at him. Blinked. The corner of his mouth quirked and he nodded toward the pasture and horses behind her. "Horses. Have you ever ridden horses before?"

"Oh. Right." *Oh God.* "No, I never have. Not much cause for them in Roxbury."

Xavier nodded, expression stoic. "I can see that." He flicked a glance over her shoulder before returning his attention to her. "Do you want a lesson?"

Stunned, she gaped at him. "Wh-what," she sputtered. "Y-you're going to give it to me?"

He shrugged. "Either me or the leprechaun sitting over there under the tree."

Her eyebrows drew together in a mock scowl even as her heart leaped at the thought of spending time with him. She desired his company more than learning to ride one of the majestic animals. "Very funny."

The familiar vulnerability crept back in like a stealthy thief, pilfering a measure of her joy. "Are you serious?"

"Yes, Gwen," he murmured and again delight rose up and warmed her like the sun's rays never could. *Gwen. He called me Gwen.* "Go put on a pair of jeans and boots, if you have any." Xavier dipped his chin in the direction of her black slacks. "I'll meet you back here in ten minutes."

She nodded briefly, then brushed past him and headed toward the house. In record time, she changed her clothes and shoes, hurried from her room, down the stairs and across the wide lawn to the pasture and stable. As she stood in the open doorway, Xavier strode down the aisle, a saddle and bridle resting on his shoulder. He paused and his steady inspection traveled from her loose curls, down her brown leather jacket, blue jeans and sneakers.

"Wait here," he ordered before spinning around and retracing his path down the breezeway toward the back of the stable. Within a couple of minutes, he returned with a pair of boots clutched in his hand.

"Here." He knelt and lowered the riding gear to the ground. The curl of his fingers beckoned her forward and she obeyed the command.

He encircled her ankle, lifted her foot and removed her sneaker. He repeated the process with the other foot and she curled her toes into the hard floor.

"These should fit. They're one of the stable hands', but I don't think she'll mind." He smoothed his palm along her arch, smoothing her white sock to ensure the garment didn't bunch and cause her any discomfort, then fit the dusty brown boot on her foot. Tenderness rippled through her in ever widening rings of delight. Warmth spread to her chest and penetrated deeper into her heart, her spirit.

"All set." Xavier patted the toe of her boot and, hoisting the saddle and bridle to his shoulder again, rose to his full height. Strange how last week he had intimidated her, but now the way he towered over her comforted her, offered security...and turned her on. Damn, she had it bad.

"Thank you," she whispered. His slight smile caused lust to knot then slowly uncoil in her stomach, shooting delicious heat to her nipples and sex. She almost suggested foregoing the lesson in favor of riding *him*.

"I chose Marian for you," he said and closed his hand around hers. "She's the gentlest mare and the most patient."

"She'll need to be with me," Gwendolyn grumbled and he flashed another of those rare smiles over his shoulder as he pulled her along. *Wow.* She exhaled a hard breath. For that smile, she would attempt to ride the wildest stallion alive.

"You might be surprised at how well you take to horseback, Gwen," he assured her with a fleeting squeeze to her fingers. He paused next to the stable doors, bent and grabbed a blanket, then continued out into the corral.

Of the four beautiful animals grazing in the field, Xavier approached a horse standing close to the fence, the slender head hanging over the top rung. The shiny, mahogany coat resembled the lustrous color of Xavier's locks. After a soft whistle and click of his tongue, he called the mare's name and she turned huge, quiet eyes to her master. He stroked her darker mane and crooned hushed praises in her ear. Gwendolyn stared at his large hands and long, elegant fingers. And swallowed a soft sigh. He'd handled her with similar gentle caresses in the heat of passion, soothing her with word and touch. And she probably trembled as Marian did under his attention.

The man had a way with the ladies. She smirked.

The horse lowered her head and nudged Xavier's pocket with her dark nose. Chuckling, he reached inside his thick black sweater and removed a carrot and a slice of apple. A pleased whinny escaped the mare before she nipped the offered food.

"Good girl," he crooned and a shiver passed down Gwen's spine and tingled in her sex. Xavier had murmured those exact words to her a couple of nights earlier. As she'd played with her pussy and he watched. She swallowed a groan.

Pay attention. Horseback riding lessons. Not sex. Not—her gaze fondled his ass in the fitted dark blue jeans as he threw the blanket over the mare's back—sex.

Minutes later, he had the saddle on the horse, the cinches tightened beneath her belly, stirrups adjusted and the bridle fastened.

"Okay, baby. Up you go." Bending low, he cupped his hands and glanced up at her. "Put your foot here and I'll hoist you up. Swing your leg over and grab the reins. I won't let anything happen to you, okay?"

She nodded, hesitant but trusting. He hadn't needed to reassure her he would care for her. She harbored no doubts on that front.

Gwendolyn followed his instructions and, in seconds, she straddled the horse's back. *Jesus.* Her stomach plummeted straight to her toes. She'd never perched on the top of the Empire State Building, but the dizzying sense of oh-my-God-please-don't-let-me-hurl-on-my-shoes had to be the same.

"Uh…"

"Easy, Gwen." Xavier chuckled and patted her calf. "I can see the whites of your eyes."

"I'm…uh…good," she stuttered. And swallowed hard. "She's awfully…um…big, isn't she?"

"Don't worry. You'll become accustomed to her. Just give it a few minutes." Again he petted her leg. "Brush her mane. Horses like to be touched, gentled. You'll lose your anxiety and she'll become more used to you."

Inhaling, she leaned forward and squeezed the reins. The horse nervously sidestepped, but Xavier immediately soothed her.

"Don't tighten up on the reins, sweetheart. There's nothing to be afraid of." She latched onto the confidence in his voice and brushed a trembling caress over the dark mane. Mimicking his tone, Gwendolyn whispered some nonsensical words and soon the pit in her stomach transformed to a shallow hole.

"You ready?" He settled his gaze on her face and the assurance in his eyes calmed her like a dozen platitudes could not.

"Ready."

For the next hour, Xavier led her and the horse through different paces. He taught her how to sit in the saddle and guide the mare, and with each small success, Gwendolyn's confidence increased. Soon her trepidation faded under the excitement of learning and feeling the animal respond to her directions. True, they never went above a slow walk but, God, it was fun!

"You're doing wonderful." She beamed and he smiled. Joy spiraled up from her stomach and mushroomed through her chest. Each smile he gifted her was better than winning the Pulitzer Prize. "Are you up for a ride?"

A thrill zinged through her. "Of course."

Xavier hooked his foot in the stirrup and swung up behind her. The leap barely stirred the horse, but Gwen's stomach dipped. Yet as soon as his chest pressed into her spine and his hips cradled her bottom, she calmed. And when he encircled her within his strong embrace to take the reins, she found sanctuary.

A low click of his tongue set them off. The horse and man flowed as one and she marveled at the beauty and strength of them. After several turns around the fenced-in pasture, he directed the mare from the corral and out into the breathtaking landscape surrounding his home.

As they trotted down a well-worn trail through the red-and-gold-painted trees, chirping birds and the muted tinkle of a far-off stream greeted them. Between the gorgeous scenery, the exhilaration of riding and the power of the man behind her, Gwendolyn was bewitched.

"Having fun?"

She tilted her head back and grinned. "God, yes." She laughed in sheer happiness. "Good," he replied, and then shocked her by planting a small kiss on the tip of her

nose. Speechless, she gaped at him before facing forward. Her heart knocked a hard

tattoo against the wall of her chest but, bit by bit, a wide grin she couldn't contain stretched her mouth. Yeah, she probably looked the fool wearing such a huge smile on her face but, dammit, she didn't care.

The horse's pace gradually slowed to a walk and she inhaled a deep breath. The clean scent of earth and Xavier's skin filled her lungs. She closed her eyes and savored the flavor of nature and man. Both seductive in their individual ways.

"Tell me about yourself, Gwen." He brushed his lips along the curve of her ear as he spoke and she squeezed her eyes tighter before lifting her lashes to stare down at his long-fingered hands, holding the reins in a loose grip. "I want to know you again."

Once more she angled her head back to regard him. "Do you?" she asked and managed not to wince at the vulnerability in those two words. But she didn't glance away. Didn't pretend as if his request for intimate knowledge of her didn't carry importance in her heart. Didn't feign as if a hidden part of her soul wasn't dancing in delight at the possibility she may be more than an available body to him.

"Yes." His solemn gaze met hers and held it. "Yes, I do."

She resumed her forward position. Where did she start? With Joshua's death? The years of guilt she'd come to terms with only last night in his arms?

"A few months after Josh's death, I assumed the role of program director at the community center. I'd been on staff there a couple of years and after Josh..." She paused and allowed the spasm of hurt to pass. "After Josh, I started spending more time there so I was thrilled when the board offered me the position."

"It was your lifesaver," he added and the wealth of understanding in his voice loosened the knot in her throat.

"Yes," she said. "It saved me. The people, the children, the purpose. I poured all of myself into the center and the kids there."

"They needed you."

She shrugged. "I'm not saying it was healthy and, in hindsight I was definitely avoiding dealing with my grief by burying myself in work, but in time I found a measure of healing."

"A measure?"

The throb of a wound covered by a fresh scab pulsed in her heart. Forgiveness was so new. Even after six years she hadn't found complete absolution and release. But unlike days ago, she now possessed faith she would one day.

"Yes," she whispered. "A measure."

He slowly nodded. "You still love him."

The statement contained no accusation or anger—no emotion at all. But the deliberate emptiness declared more than a speech.

Gwendolyn tipped her head back to stare at the crisp blue sky. Two birds soaring through the clouds snagged her attention. One hovered a short distance behind the other as if promising to catch its mate if it fell. She yearned for the same security, commitment and trust. The assurance that when she faltered, love would buoy her up.

"I'll always miss him," she stated, choosing her words with care. "He was my best friend, my first relationship. He gave me the stability my mother never did. For his friendship he will always hold a special place in my heart." She tightened her grip on the saddle horn as the last part—the hardest part—of her admission arrived. "But I don't hold a torch for him. Nothing is preventing me from caring for someone again. I want to...love."

"But you haven't been with anyone." Xavier shifted behind her and pressed closer. The stiff column of his cock pushed into her lower back and, though he only held her close, liquid need pooled between her legs. "Your actions don't show you're ready, Gwen."

She lowered her head. How could she respond to that? Not with the truth.

"Seven years," he wondered aloud. "You said it'd been seven years since you'd been with a man. Joshua has been dead for six. Why, sweetheart?"

Dust coated her mouth and her pulse echoed inside her head like a bass drum. She swiped her tongue over her dry lips and filled her lungs to respond, but nothing emerged. Again, words eluded her. Somehow, *I couldn't abide having sex with your brother any longer since every encounter left me sick with guilt, as if I were cheating on you instead of him,* didn't seem like the appropriate thing to say.

"Gwen?"

"We agreed to be celibate a year before we married." Partly true. She'd requested it and Josh had agreed. At the time, she'd been shocked at his acquiescence. But had he suspected her love for Xavier even then?

"I always thought Josh was a saint," he murmured, switching the leather reins to one hand and lifting the other to her cheek. A gust of breath shuddered from between her lips as he trailed the backs of his fingers over her skin. Her lashes fluttered closed as love squeezed her heart. "Now I have clear evidence. He must've had a fucking halo to agree. There's no way I could have you and not be inside you at any given opportunity."

Molten heat throbbed in her core as if the hard thrust of his cock filled her, stretched her. The rhythmic rise and fall of the horse beneath her did nothing to alleviate the ache. The mare's gait inflamed the need, stoked it until her breathing grew shallow and she shivered with the longing to touch and be touched.

Xavier called to the horse and drew back on the reins. As the mare halted, Gwendolyn glanced around a lovely glen with a small brook running next to it. The quiet peace of the oasis called to her as Xavier dismounted, and she didn't utter a protest when he gripped her waist and lifted her from the saddle.

"This is beautiful." She smiled at him over her shoulder. Several quick steps brought her to the clear water. It babbled over the dark bed of the creek and the cleverly placed stepping stones leading to the stretch of vibrant green on the other side. "How did you find it?"

He stuffed his hands in the front pockets of his jeans. "I've spent a lot of time out here." Again, the carefully neutral voice.

She turned away from the idyllic scene and studied him. Though he stood motionless, power emanated from his still form. His vitality tugged at her like a siren song. She'd crashed on the shores of his desire, had drowned under the waves of his passion. And she longed for a repeat performance.

Gwendolyn's gaze clashed with his narrowed regard. "My turn."

Xavier lifted both brows, but remained silent. Even when she retraced her steps across the grass, halted before him and raised a hand to his face—the left side. She gave him credit. He almost managed to stifle his flinch as she neared the scar. If she hadn't been scrutinizing him so closely, she would've missed the nearly imperceptible jerk.

She stroked his clenched jaw and stubble the sharpest razor couldn't remove grazed her knuckles.

"Your turn?" he questioned, his voice a low rumble in the still glen. "To ask about you," she explained.

With a sigh of delight, she thrust her fingers under the bound tail of hair at his neck and cupped his scalp. The black fan of his lashes flickered, but his eyes didn't close. His faint hiss smacked of approval, not distress.

"You have beautiful hair, Xavier. I remember being so jealous of it. It didn't seem fair God gave you—a man—such thick, gorgeous manageable hair while cursing me with the wild mop I had—have."

A corner of his full lips quirked at her disgruntled complaint. "I've always loved your hair," he murmured.

Lord. She gasped, her eyes almost rolling to the back of her head as he twisted a handful in a gentle but firm grip. He'd tugged on the curls in the same manner when kissing her. Who would've guessed nerves in the scalp were connected to the clit? A little-known medical mystery.

"I used to have fantasies about it. About fisting a handful of your curls around my cock and fucking your hair." A self-deprecating smile curved his mouth. "Depraved, isn't it?"

Hot. Erotic. Orgasmic. But no, not depraved. "You never let on..." She swallowed in an attempt to wet her mouth which had gone dry as the Sahara. "When?"

Xavier dropped his hand and the suddenness of the action left her alone, bereft. As if she'd been abruptly shoved into the freezing cold after warming herself in front of a comforting, lovely fire. His gaze—

which had burned with desire—cooled. A door had slammed in his head, locking her out of his thoughts. "Long past the time I should've."

"What does that—"

"What did you want to ask me?"

She snapped her mouth shut, the questions trapped. For a long second, they examined each other, the past sandwiched between them like a fucked-up ménage.

Finally, she flexed her fingertips against his head. "Why do you wear your hair tied back? I haven't seen it loose except for last night..."

She sucked in a hard breath. Held it.

All sound in the glade fell away until an unnatural, thick silence reigned. Nothing moved. Not the soaring birds. Not the gurgling brook. Not Xavier.

Her throat burned from the lack of oxygen. But it couldn't compare to the utter agony in his eyes. *Jesus.* Air exploded from her lungs and she snatched her hand from his hair and cradled it in her other palm. No one should hurt like that.

"Never mind." She shook her head. "You don't have—"

"I'm a monster," he said. And she could have wept at the conviction in the stark statement. "This way no one forgets." If possible, his features tautened even more. "Do you know why Evelyn and I broke up?" He released a humorless bark of laughter. "I walked in on her having sex with another man. And still I didn't have the balls to end our relationship. She did. Because she couldn't stand to look at me. Apparently pulling my hair forward to hide my face while we fucked wasn't cutting it any longer."

* * * * *

Xavier bit back a curse and told himself to shut the fuck up. Especially when a bright sheen dampened her brown gaze. He jerked his head away from the sight of her pity and squeezed his eyes shut. Joy, laughter, passion—those were the emotions he loved to see light her lovely face. He even preferred anger to pity.

For a short precious while the acidic bitterness he'd existed with for a year had loosened its hold. After last night, he'd been stupid as shit to surrender to the tentative fantasy that the hurt, shame and anger were in the past, burned away by the welcoming heat of Gwendolyn's arms and body.

When she'd kissed each of his scars with gentle tenderness, he'd gritted his teeth and tightened his jaw. At first he'd wanted to rip free of his binds and shove her away. He hadn't wanted to be reminded of the network of puckered flesh marring his chest and abdomen. But with each pass of her lips, his body had hardened and his heart— his soul—had softened.

She'd accomplished the impossible. She'd made him forget.

But now, as the old emotions of pain, rejection and loneliness returned like a millstone around his neck, truth slapped him in the face with the clarity of an ice-cold bucket of water.

Gwendolyn might—*might*—be able to look past his disfigurement, but no one else would. Evelyn hadn't managed it. And while he may be capable of coming to grips with and accepting that realization, a very ugly, cowardly fear still remained burrowed deep within his psyche. Would the day arrive when Gwendolyn regretted having him by her side? When she would be ashamed to walk next to him in public where people pointed and whispered? The thought of her regret—her shame—he couldn't abide.

Nor could he allow the intimacy of the past two nights to blind him to the reason she stood in this place with him. He'd blackmailed her. Yes, she cared about him but affection and love weren't the same things. And in this idyllic setting, away from the outside world, he could so easily delude himself into pretending they were identical.

Evelyn had taught him the harsh lesson of believing in fairy tales.

"That bitch."

The furious growl startled him. He swung his head back to stare down at Gwendolyn's infuriated features. Her eyebrows formed a deep vee and the sensual curve of her mouth had flattened into an angry slash.

"That disloyal, traitorous bitch."

He shrugged. "Could you really blame—" "Stop it."

He snapped his jaw shut, shocked into speechlessness by her vehemence.

"What, Xavier? Because of one heartless woman—and I use the term 'woman' lightly—you use your face as some kind of 'I'll fuck you before you fuck me'?" She thumped a balled fist into his chest. "How dare you."

Stunned, he couldn't respond to the accusation or the language. What the hell was she talking about?

"I don't give a damn about your ex or your *friends*." She sneered the word, her disgust telegraphing her opinion of those he once called by the same name. "How they react out of their petty shallowness is *their* shame, not yours. What pisses me off is how you wield your appearance like some kind of weapon to prove to them their cruelty doesn't hurt. When it clearly does. Don't deny it," she snapped, glaring at him when he parted his lips.

"Xavier." The ferocity suffusing her face bled away. Gwendolyn shifted forward, cupped his cheek and swept a thumb over his damaged skin. The caress rocked him, cauterized the bleeding wound in his soul. He shuddered.

"Xavier," she repeated and he opened eyes he hadn't realized he'd closed. "No, you're not perfect anymore. And I thank God for it." Her voice cracked then steadied. "I love this scar. It means you survived. You're alive and here with me. You could be—"

"Baby," he murmured and dragged her into his arms. The fresh, vanilla scent of her shampoo surrounded him as he buried his face in her light curls. Her arms encircled his torso and squeezed so hard his ribs bleated a faint objection.

Shame again assailed him. But this time he attributed the guilt to his selfishness and ingratitude. Since the accident, he'd railed at God for leaving him in such a broken, lonely state. His resentment had colored every aspect of a life he used to enjoy. Even after the grief of his father's death passed, his anger had never extinguished.

Gwendolyn's compassion and honesty revealed who he'd become. Someone so consumed with all he'd lost he'd never appreciated everything he still had. Someone so embittered he'd measured his value by others' opinions and on something as shallow and fleeting as appearance. Someone so cold he'd extorted the body of a woman who would have freely given him her friendship.

Someone his father would have been ashamed of.

"I'm so sorry," he rasped, unsure if he apologized to her or the man who had taught him the meaning of manhood and integrity.

She tightened her embrace. The wild curls he adored brushed his chin and cheek as she tipped her head back to search his face. "Prove it," she whispered.

Xavier released her. Inhaled. And lifted his arms behind his head. In seconds, he freed his hair from the rubber band. He didn't miss the slight widening of her eyes or the wonder that entered their chocolate-brown depths as the heavy strands fell forward to frame his face.

Her delight scoured away the last of his doubt and trepidation. Damn if he didn't want to preen under her blatant admiration.

She rose on tiptoe and pressed soft, full lips to his. He captured her mouth and slanted his head to bury his tongue deeper. Her sweetness sucked him under and like a drug addict after his first hit, he would always chase this woman for more of her special, addictive taste.

He tore his mouth away and slicked his tongue across his bottom lip, savoring her flavor. A groan rumbled from his throat. How could he *want* this much?

"Turn around, baby," he ordered, gripping her waist. Without the slightest hesitation, she complied and allowed him to guide her to one of the towering trees filling the grove. After flattening her hands on the thick trunk, he covered her hands with his and lowered his head to nuzzle the curve of her ear.

"So beautiful," he said and nipped the earlobe. "So strong." A kiss to the skin behind her ear. "So generous."

"Xavier." She shivered.

"Shhh... I have you." Her jacket didn't prove a barrier as he slid his hands up her arms, down the sides of her body and under her shirt. His cock jerked in his pants as he cradled her full breasts. She shuddered in his arms, a sharp cry breaking free as he pinched the stiff nipples.

Her hips bucked and he ground his dick into the sweet curves of her jeans-covered ass. Shit, he needed inside her. Bad.

He swept a hand down her stomach. The firm muscles contracted under his touch and her gasp echoed in the quiet glade. In seconds, he'd loosened the button, lowered the zipper and found heaven.

"Oh fuck," he growled. "You're so wet, baby." He dragged two fingers through the smooth folds until he encountered the engorged bundle of nerves crowning the top of her sex. "I'll never get tired of feeling you cream for me."

Placing an open-mouthed kiss to the underside of her jaw, he razed her skin with his teeth as he circled her clit with damp fingers. Over and over, he teased and stroked the swollen button, drawing more erotic cries from her throat. He released his hold on her breast, shoved her jeans and panties down her hips and thrust two fingers in her rippling pussy.

"Oh God, please," she pleaded, her back arching. She curled her fingers against the bark of the tree.

"Dammit, Gwendolyn," he whispered, "you're so tight, so hot." The strong walls of her sex clamped down on his fingers and milked them as if they were his cock. His breath labored in his chest and, as he withdrew and drove back inside the snug channel, his cock throbbed, his balls drew tight and the base of his spine tingled with impending release.

A broken sob escaped her lips and she quaked in his embrace. Every grind of her hips as she rode his fingers and each "please" she whispered were like gifts. No woman had ever responded to his touch like Gwendolyn did. Even before the accident had ripped his face open. Not even Evelyn had unraveled with such uninhibited pleasure as this woman pleading for him to make her come. Her abandon was every bit as sexy as her mouth on his cock. Maybe more.

"I have you, baby." He pressed another kiss to her jaw and neck. "Come for me. Hard. Don't hold anything back," he demanded and plied her clit with firm passes of his thumb. Her pussy received short, steady thrusts and her hips quickened, following the rhythm he set. Her constant litany of cries incited his pace and lust. "That's it, baby. Fuck my fingers." He murmured his approval as Gwendolyn spread her slim thighs and rode his hand with abrupt, rough rolls.

Her sex coated his fingers in her essence. That's what he wanted. What he needed. Muttering a harsh curse, he executed a rapid succession of firm strokes to her clit with the pad of his thumb and plunged his fingers deep into her spasming vise of a pussy.

Gwendolyn quaked in his embrace, climaxing with a scream that echoed in the air.

And he loved it.

"Take it, baby," he urged, strumming her clit and thrusting faster into the milking channel. "Don't stop, Gwendolyn. Take every bit of it." For several long moments, she convulsed in his arms, riding out the storm until only small shudders and whimpers remained.

With a raw moan, he removed his touch from her quivering flesh and lifted his fingers to his lips. The last thing he wanted was to abandon her pussy, but the need to taste what he'd fingered rode him just as hard. Sliding the damp digits deep into his mouth, he sucked her juice clean.

As she sagged in his arms, Xavier encircled her hips with an arm to hold her up.

His cock demanded release. He was almost crazed with it.

He shifted her body and guided her hips farther back. With a hard tug, he pulled her jeans lower and then pushed her legs wider apart. Her beautiful, round ass kept a stranglehold on his attention. In several hasty movements he attacked the zipper of his pants and freed his aching cock. The rigid length pulsed in his fist. Shifting forward, he gripped her hip and pressed the swollen cock head to her shadowed cleft and slowly— savoring the initial sensation of flesh against flesh—surged upward into her pussy.

Her ass cheeks parted with the thrust of his dick and surrounded his hard flesh. *Oh fuck.* Lust grabbed his balls and squeezed, shoving him closer to the edge of orgasm. Gwendolyn whimpered and circled her hips, stroking his cock. He tightened his grip on her hip and she complied with the unspoken command, bowing deeper at the waist.

"God yes, baby," he whispered. He bent his knees, drew back then thrust forward into the sweetest, hottest fist of flesh. He groaned, bent over Gwendolyn and pressed his forehead into her shoulder blade. Her tight sheath created a perfect, heated glove for his cock. One day he wanted her breasts like this. He withdrew and thrust forward again. Except on the upstroke, she would fit her plump lips around his head and suck the spill of his cum. The thought caused his hips to jerk harder, piston faster, his cock to sink deeper.

Sounds of sex filled the air. The slap of flesh against flesh. The soft cries and harsh groans. The wet suction and release as his cock fucked her pussy.

"Oh God," she sobbed. "Xavier, please."

His breath burned his chest and throat. Sweat prickled under his arms and at the back of his neck. The base of his spine tingled and his balls tightened as release threatened to steal his mind. *Together.* He thrust his dick into her pussy. *We'll do this together.* Dipped a hand between her legs and pressed his thumb to her clit. Hard.

For the second time, Gwendolyn came apart in his arms.

"Fuck," he rasped and her accompanying moan contained all the need and lust raging inside him.

He jerked back, reached inside his jacket pocket, snatched a tissue free and covered his cock head while stroking the hard length. An animalistic growl rumbled from his chest, catching him by surprise as the first jet of semen erupted from his dick. Raw and primal, the power of the orgasm reduced him to single-syllable swear words and grunts of ecstasy.

As the last shudder eased over his body, he closed his eyes and turned his head. His cheek rested against her shoulder. He breathed her in.

God, it didn't get any better than this. "Take me home."

He stood corrected.

Take me home. The words echoed in his head as he and Gwendolyn cleaned up and readjusted their clothing. They vibrated through him the short ride back to the house. Even if the words had been a slip of the tongue or a turn of phrase, she'd thought of his house as "home".

Hope he hadn't allowed to take root sprouted in his heart. And for the first time, he didn't strike it back down.

They hurried through cooling Marian down, brushing her free of any dirt and tangles, and stored the riding gear against the rear wall of the stable. Gwendolyn appeared as eager as he to finish the task and continue what they'd shared in the quiet glade. To reinforce the small bridge of trust and healing they had erected.

Hell, he just wanted her like a fat kid wanted cake.

His lips quirked. Not exactly romantic, but damn, he couldn't wait to lick every inch of her coffee-and-cream skin. He wanted to gorge himself on her again and then go back for another round.

Again with the gluttony analogies.

Xavier glanced down at her as they climbed the shallow steps to the porch and approached the front door. As she reached for the handle, he covered her hand with his. She paused and, glancing up, arched an eyebrow. He didn't immediately respond to the silent question, but instead brushed her temple with a light kiss.

"Forgive me," he whispered. The words had swelled in his chest and spilled out before he realized the intent to utter them.

Her forehead crinkled with a frown. "Okay," she agreed, then paused. "What am I forgiving you for?"

He smiled and shook his head. "Most people would ask the question first." His smile fell away and he grazed the backs of his fingers over the delicate line of her jaw. "For hurting you. Never have I thought of you as less than the beautiful, proud, giving woman you are. But I know my actions didn't express that. I disrespected you out of my own insecurity and bitterness because I didn't believe you could possibly want me. I regret my fucking bargain now. More than you know."

"I don't."

He stiffened, certain he'd heard wrong. She faced him and tilted her head back to meet his eyes. The tenderness in her brown gaze set his heart beating in a pounding, deafening rhythm.

"Every feverish hour spent driving here, every hurt feeling, every urge to drop-kick you," she smiled at his snort, "was worth your 'fucking bargain'. If it brought me to this moment with you, I'd do it over again in a heartbeat."

Jesus. He squeezed his eyes shut as so many feelings churned in his chest and surged up to his throat. Wonder. Hope. Fear. They choked him, driving the breath from his body.

"Baby—"

"Xavier."

He jerked his head up at the melodious, cultured voice. On some vague level, he was aware of Gwendolyn's small gasp as she whirled to face the open door behind them. The sound reached him from a great distance as everything around him faded to an indistinct blur and only the slender dark-haired woman standing in the doorway remained in sharp focus.

The last time he'd seen her, she'd stood in their apartment, naked and trembling under the silk robe she'd dragged on after he'd caught her having sex with a man in their bed.

"Evelyn."

CHAPTER NINE

"No, dear Beast," said Beauty, "you must not die. Alas! I thought I had only a friendship for you, but the grief I now feel convinces me that I cannot live without you."

—*Beauty and the Beast*

"Do I believe in happily ever after? No. Do I want to believe? God, yes."—
Gwendolyn Sinclair

Evelyn.

Gwendolyn stared at the elegant, beautiful woman standing in the foyer. The slight smile curving her lips and the gleam in her sky-blue eyes emanated a confident assurance of her welcome. And return.

At some point after she'd appeared, their unlikely trio had moved into the house. The transition was a foggy blur. Only the steadily increasing dread that leached the joy from Gwen's heart remained in sharp focus.

Here stood the woman Xavier had been prepared to marry. And she didn't need to be a Rhodes Scholar to deduce if Evelyn had shown up at his home unannounced, clad in a formfitting dress with a price tag probably exceeding more than her entire wardrobe, the ex had arrived to change her status.

She logged a mental comparison of her windblown hair, loose jacket, jeans and scuffed boots to Evelyn's smooth chignon, wraparound sheath and knee-high stiletto boots…and wished she hadn't. God, she must resemble a street urchin next to Evelyn's lady-of-the-manor appearance.

Evelyn moved forward in a sensuous glide, her smile deepening with an increasing intimacy. Gwendolyn alternated between longing to weep and desiring to claw the woman's eyes out. He's mine, she wanted to shout. You forfeited your future with him and now he's mine. But she remained quiet. Even when the statuesque beauty bypassed her as if she weren't there and approached a motionless Xavier. Shock, fury and grief had stolen her voice, leaving her powerless except to watch the drama unfold before her.

She pivoted, unable to not watch. Helplessness bound her arms to her sides and glued her feet to the foyer floor as the man she loved reunited with his former fiancée.

"Xavier," Evelyn greeted him again in a warm voice just short of a purr. "It's so good to see you."

Stone-faced, eyes shards of flint, he'd reverted to the cold stranger of a week ago. He closed the front door with a decisive thud, his gaze never leaving Evelyn's face. His closed expression revealed neither anger nor welcome, resentment nor delight. Just…nothing.

"Evelyn," he repeated. "What are you doing here?"

The hard tone halted her progress and she stiffened, the arms she'd lifted descending back to her sides. Apparently, she had expected Xavier to receive her with open arms. With herculean effort, Gwendolyn didn't cross the room and squeeze between the former lovers in order to protect Xavier from this woman's selfishness and conceit. She'd cast him aside as if the years they'd been together hadn't mattered—like he hadn't mattered. Like she hadn't inflicted deeper, more horrible scars than a mere mark on his face.

Yes, Evelyn had wreaked far more damage. She'd executed the death blow to his confidence, colored how he viewed the world and people in it. And her wound had been worse because the strike had come from someone he'd trusted. He'd loved.

What a fool.

If she ever had Xavier's love, his trust, Gwendolyn would harm herself before causing him pain.

"I came to see you. I've missed you," she said and Gwendolyn almost believed the sincerity lacing the claim. Evelyn placed a manicured hand on his chest, over his heart, and Gwendolyn's nails bit into her palms, the sting a sharp reminder she couldn't slap the offending touch away.

"Really." He arched an eyebrow. "How did you know I was here?" "Your mother told me."

A twist of his lips. "Of course." Finally, he stepped back. Evelyn's hand fell from him and the fist around Gwendolyn's heart released its tight grip. "Well, you're here. Say what you came to get off your chest so I can get on with my day."

If possible, more steel entered her spine. But her tone remained even, confident. "Can we have a little," she turned and pinned Gwendolyn with a hard stare, "privacy? This is between you and me."

As if remembering she stood there with them, Xavier lifted his penetrating gaze to her. Until then, she retained a tiny hope he would... God, she didn't know. Tell Evelyn to get the hell out? Tell her...tell her he loved someone new? Like her?

One look in his eyes and she threw those hopes away like yesterday's garbage. He intended on meeting with Evelyn. And after that?

"I'll head upstairs," she murmured and trapped a primal scream in her chest. Still...why weren't the pristine hardwood floors smeared with her blood as it pumped from the ragged gash in her heart? "Excuse me."

She spun on her heel, crossed the foyer and climbed the steps. The deal entailed seven days, not a lifetime. No promises of happily ever after.

Too bad her foolish heart had started to believe in them.

"Wasn't that Joshua's fiancée?"

* * * * *

Xavier folded his arms and stared at the woman who—at one time—he'd planned a life with. Seven months hadn't wrought any changes. Still beautiful, classy, sexy. Still unable to look him fully in the face.

No, their time apart hadn't brought changes in her, but it had worked wonders for him. Her sudden appearance should have ignited a chain reaction of anger, insecurity, resentment and pain. Instead it elicited only curiosity and irritation over the interruption in his day.

Gwendolyn had done that for him. Incredibly, her unconditional acceptance had healed him. An image of her eyes as she caressed his scar and admitted she thanked God for it rose to mind.

She'd performed a miracle and he had only to peer inside himself to marvel at the wonder of its power.

"Gwendolyn." He supplied her name, resting his spine against the mantel. "And no, since my brother died six years ago, Gwendolyn is not Joshua's fiancée."

Evelyn flicked her fingers in an impatient gesture. "You know what I mean, Xavier." She frowned. "What is she doing here?"

"The better question," he countered, cocking his head, "is what are you doing here? She was invited. You, on the other hand, were not."

Her calm, sophisticated façade wavered for a quick moment before reassuming its placid, pleasant lines. Too late, though. He'd glimpsed the annoyance beneath. Inside he smiled. Good. He had no desire to be vindictive, but now she grasped he wasn't some desperate, lovesick sap, thankful to be blessed by her presence.

The woman who held the power to bring him to his knees occupied a room upstairs. And the need to be with her ached like a limb had been amputated.

"I don't have the time or patience for twenty questions," he growled. "Spill it or leave."

"I deserve your anger." She drew closer to him, her clear blue eyes dark with regret. "Yell at me. Call me a bitch. I've earned every bit of your resentment."

"How magnanimous of you."

"Honey," she whispered and settled a slender hand on his biceps.

He unfolded his arms and dropped his hands to his sides. But his aversion to her touch didn't deter her. As in the foyer, she splayed her fingers over his chest. At one time the same gesture and sexy pout could have wheedled anything out of him. Now the effect only left an urge to pluck her hand away.

"I know I hurt you. I made a horrible mistake. But please, give me a chance to make it up to you. I've been miserable without you. We were so good together and I was a fool to throw our relationship away so carelessly. Please," she pleaded again, voice soft. She lowered her gaze to his chest, the very picture of demure contrition. "Give me...us...another try. We are worth it."

"Evelyn, look at me."

Confusion crossed her lovely features at his low command. "What do—" "Look at me."

A spasm of what he could only define as dismay rippled across her face. She peeked at his scar, glanced away. It should have stabbed deep, her distaste. And on some level, it did sting. The horror-tinged expressions on people's faces as they stared into his would most likely never cease to hurt. But dampening their repugnance would be the memory of Gwendolyn, trailing kisses over every inch of the puckered flesh, worshipping his scar as if it were precious instead of disgusting.

He could bear the slight pain with that vision offsetting it. "Xavier, I—"

"Exactly what I figured," he murmured. "How can we have a future when you can't even bear to look me in the face? Do you think it's going to disappear?" He encircled her wrist, lifted her palm to his cheek and set her skin against it. "This is me."

She snatched her hand away as if the mark had singed her flesh and shuffled backward, the awkward gesture incongruous with the urbane image she projected. She rubbed her thumb over her palm as if she could wipe the touch away. He doubted his ex-fiancée was conscious of the nervous action, but it shouted the truth to him.

"Don't say that," she ordered as she turned from him. With a deep inhalation of breath, she gathered her composure before confronting him again. "It is not you."

"You're right," he agreed and straightened off the mantel, shoving his hands in his pockets. "It isn't. I'm more than this scar. I'm a man who still breathes, still works, is learning to laugh again and still loves. And wants to be loved. Deserves to be loved."

"I do love you!"

He shook his head at her husky cry. "You couldn't have walked away so easily if you did."

Fury twisted her features and a hint of pain penetrated the angry mask. It dawned on him like the morning sun rising over the horizon. Evelyn did care for him. As much as her heart was capable. Though a product of the same self-entitled upbringing he'd been reared in, she hadn't benefited from the love, patience and humility his parents—especially his father—had passed on to him. Those qualities had counterbalanced the elitism that existed among his peers.

He sighed and tunneled his fingers through his hair, gripped a handful at his nape before dropping his arm back to his side. "I'm not being vengeful. And I'm not trying to hurt you—"

"But you are!" she shouted. "I cheated on you. I'm sorry. More than you'll ever know. And I can understand you want to punish me for it, but for how long? I'm asking you not to do this."

"Yes, you cheated." Yet as much as her betrayal grated, if their love had been strong enough, even that could've been forgiven in time. "But it wasn't the act as much as the reason behind it." He hardened his voice when she cut her eyes away from him. Even now she couldn't—refused to—face the truth. "My face repulsed you so much the thought of making love to me drove you into the arms of another man. That's not leaving the toilet seat up. It's not something we can work on in counseling."

"Xavier."

"Don't." He didn't have it in him to be cruel. At some point during the past week, love had dulled the sharp edge of his anger toward this woman. How could he hold a grudge against Evelyn when her actions—though like a knife in his heart at the time— had propelled him to this place, this time?

To Gwendolyn.

If she hadn't ended their engagement, he would have been trapped in a loveless marriage with a woman who couldn't bear his touch, much less love him.

Gwendolyn would have never betrayed him. Never would have abandoned— The truth struck him with the force of a blow to the jaw.

She loved him. Gwendolyn loved him.

Every gesture, word and smile during the past week flew through his mind at breakneck speed. His gut clenched. His throat worked as it struggled to swallow the tennis ball-sized lump of cautious excitement. Her laughter as she teased him. Her voice as she'd called him beautiful. Her uninhibited response to his touch. Her eyes as she'd thanked God for his scar, his life.

"Shit," he whispered.

Awe filled him. Along with a joy so precious, so scary in its sheer power, his heart drummed in his chest, drowning out everything but its bass reverberations. Evelyn's lips moved, but not one word penetrated the roar deafening his ears. He didn't care. If it didn't involve escaping this room and getting to the woman upstairs as soon as possible, he didn't give a fuck.

"It's over, Evelyn." The statement brooked no further discussion. "There is no going back. And I don't want to. I'll walk you out."

He strode forward and with a light but unyielding grip, guided her toward the study door.

"It's her, isn't it?" she snapped, jerking her arm from his hold. A sharp bark of laughter pierced the room as her lip curled in a humorless smile. "It's always been her."

He frowned. "What are you talking about?"

"Give me some credit," she said bitterly. "Did you believe I didn't know there was always someone else?"

"What are you talking about?" he repeated, baffled. He held his palms out, clueless. "I never cheated on you."

"Right," she scoffed. "I slept with another man, but he didn't have my heart. Yet, then again, I never had yours. Not completely. In some ways, your infidelity was worse." When he shook his head, she emitted another of those abrupt cracks of laughter. "I noticed the way you watched her, Xavier. Ever solicitous of your brother's fiancée. Always attentive. God, I was such an idiot."

Again shock paralyzed him. Her accusations bounced against his skull like a demented ping-pong ball. Jesus. Had he withheld part of himself from Evelyn the years they'd been together? He hadn't...

Yes. He had. For more than half his life, Gwendolyn had been an integral presence. First as a little sister, then as a friend and finally...finally as the woman who had healed his soul with her loveliness, laughter and light.

The woman he loved.

Damn. He rubbed a hand over his face and curved it around the back of his neck.

Gwendolyn had become entrenched in his heart as a nine-year-old child, and as she'd grown, she claimed a bit more. And then a bit more. Until he couldn't remember a time when she hadn't owned a piece of him.

All these years he'd consigned his desire for her as a physical reaction—an inappropriate hunger for the woman who'd belonged to his brother. But the tenderness, the need to hear her voice, touch her, inhale her vanilla scent, hear her sweet laughter... Those things exceeded simple "attraction".

Maybe on some unconscious level, he'd acknowledged he loved

her. And that small part of him hadn't permitted him to give his whole heart and affection to another woman...because they'd already belonged to Gwendolyn.

He lifted his gaze to Evelyn's face, drawn in tight lines of anger. "I'm sorry. I didn't realize."

"Is that supposed to make it better?" She huffed, disgusted, and waved his apology off. "I don't need your 'I'm sorry'. I walked into our relationship with my eyes wide open, believing we could be happy. And we would have been."

"Maybe for a little while," he conceded gently. "But not indefinitely. In the end, you would've been hurt far worse. And hated me for it."

"I was willing to take the chance."

Silence loomed between them as they faced each other, former lovers, almost life partners. The past weighed heavily on his heart and he was ready to shut the door on it and go to the woman who was his future.

"It's ironic," Evelyn murmured. "Neither of you realized how the other felt and yet you somehow ended up together anyway."

He stiffened. Shit. He'd woken up in an alternate universe and every time he turned around, another revelation kicked him in the teeth. "Explain."

She hesitated. After several tense moments, the stubborn set of her mouth softened and she sighed. Her lashes lowered until only a narrow blue strip remained visible. "The night Joshua died I overheard Gwendolyn speaking to him. She..." Evelyn paused, cleared her throat. "She broke off their engagement—"

"She what?" He hadn't heard right. He couldn't have. Gwendolyn had never mentioned calling off the wedding.

Evelyn nodded and met his gaze. "She broke off their engagement," she repeated. "Joshua erupted, called her names. Accused her of loving you and she didn't deny it."

"Oh God," he whispered, his breath a harsh razor over the lining of his throat even as a fist of regret tightened his chest, shutting off all air to his lungs. Like a drunken sailor, he spun around, lurched toward the front door and flung it open.

"Let yourself out," he tossed over his shoulder as he crossed the foyer and bounded up the stairs at a dead run.

CHAPTER TEN

"I was suffering in silence...only the love of a maiden willing to accept me as I was could transform me back into my real self. My dearest! I'll be so happy if you'll marry me."

—Beauty and the Beast

"I love you."—Xavier St. James

The minutes ticked by like hours. Logic reasoned that twenty-three—Gwendolyn glanced at the gold-framed clock on the bedside table—twenty-four minutes had passed since she'd left Xavier with Evelyn. But the torturous seconds might as well as have been an eternity.

After the first ten minutes, she'd abandoned her vigil on the window seat. Evelyn's sleek Aston Martin parked in the circular drive hadn't moved and every second the vehicle remained impelled Gwendolyn closer and closer to the edge of paranoia.

Her imagination had supplied several scenarios...each one worse than the last. Xavier hearing Evelyn out, then escorting her to the door.

Xavier listening to Evelyn's pleas of forgiveness, accepting them then kissing her farewell before she left the house.

Xavier wiping away Evelyn's tears as she begged him to come back to her, him telling her of course he had missed her desperately, and then the pair surrendering to passion right on the floor.

"Damn." She groaned and tunneled her fingers through her hair, sweeping the curls away from her face. Like a glutton for punishment, she stepped in front of the wall mirror and stared. The curls tumbled down in a wild, burnished mass. So unlike Evelyn's smooth, stylish chignon she cringed.

The other woman embodied the cultured, moneyed world Xavier moved and lived in. She was the accomplished hostess he required for business dinners. The connected socialite who could trace her family roots back to the Mayflower.

And she...she was...

The woman who loved him.

In the mirror, her brown eyes narrowed, turned fierce.

Yes, Evelyn might belong to Boston's elite, but Xavier belonged to *her*. She could give him laughter, passion, tenderness and a swift kick in the ass if he needed one. In the last week, she'd done all of those things and, God willing, she would continue for the next fifty plus years.

Shaking off the melancholy and self-pity, she wheeled away from the mirror and headed toward the bedroom door. Twenty-four—another quick glance at the clock—twenty-eight minutes should be long enough for the other woman to unload her guilt and apologies. It'd better be, because she sure as hell refused to stand by and hand-deliver Xavier to his ex without coming clean herself. Time to admit everything. About Joshua. His death.

Her love for him.

The thought of his reaction caused a vise to grip her stomach and tighten. But she breathed through it. She couldn't—*wouldn't*—allow anxiety to deter her. At least if he sent her home, it wouldn't be as the coward she'd been for so many years—first with Joshua and then with him. She'd been held captive by fear and insecurity far too long. Xavier wasn't her mother. He wasn't—

The door flew open. The wood bounced against the wall and her heart lodged in her throat. She bit back a squeak, but couldn't prevent her eyes from widening at Xavier's sudden and dramatic appearance.

His name hovered on her lips but remained there, unspoken, as he entered the room and shut the door behind him with a quiet click more ominous than his arrival.

Shock hadn't released its cold grip. She remained a frozen statue, lips parted, eyes as wide as saucers. The austere lines of his face revealed nothing. But his eyes. *Whoa.* They betrayed what seethed behind the stern mask. The green fire blazed and for an insane moment it was as if flames licked over her face and throat.

What the hell had happened downstairs?

"I have a question and I want you to answer it," he said quietly. An uneasy shiver skated down her spine. "Yes or no. Do you understand?"

She nodded, loath to disagree given his present state.

"Did you call off the wedding and break off the engagement to Joshua the night he died?"

She gasped. Nausea cramped her stomach and rolled over her like an enormous tidal wave, threatening to suck her under. Black, fuzzy dots swarmed her peripheral vision. The air in the room thinned, disappeared and, damn, she was going to faint.

"Gwendolyn." The razor-sharp voice lashed out at her and cleared her head like an arctic blast. In seconds, the dark edges in her vision receded and she could breathe again. Her heart slowed to a somewhat normal rate, but the nausea lingered, as did the twisted knots in her stomach.

She met his bright stare. "Yes."

"Why?"

Why? Moments ago she'd been ready to confess all, but now...now that the time had arrived dread filled her chest like a block of concrete. The courage she had gathered trickled away like water circling down a drain. God, he had the power to crush her.

"I couldn't." She shook her head and held her arms out, palms up, as if she didn't have anything else to offer him. "I'd convinced myself I could go through with the wedding and the marriage, but sitting there at the rehearsal dinner, I knew I couldn't. Not when..." She faltered and her heart pounded so hard, she feared it would burst out of her chest. "When I couldn't give him what he deserved in a wife."

"What, Gwendolyn?" He stepped forward. His gaze bored into her, commanding the truth. "What did he deserve?"

"Love. Honesty. Fidelity," she confessed, allowing her arms to fall to her sides. "I might not have betrayed him physically, but he didn't own my heart. I told you we had agreed to abstain from sex a year before our marriage. The truth was I couldn't have sex with Josh any longer. It damaged something inside me every time. Not only was I deceiving him, but the guilt sickened me." She splayed her fingers over her abdomen as if even now shame churned in her belly. "In the long run, I would have made him miserable and I couldn't cause him any more pain. Even though I didn't love him as a lover and wife, he was still the best friend I had."

"Who did you love?" Xavier moved so fast her breath snagged in her throat. One moment he'd been several feet away and the next he loomed over her, her face cradled between his large palms. He stroked her cheekbones with his thumbs, the caress firm and demanding. "Tell me, Gwen."

Gwen. Joy surged, hard and fierce. He'd called her Gwen. "You," she whispered. "I love you."

He moaned her name and crushed his lips to hers. Teeth collided, tongues tangled, lips suckled. He feasted on her like a starving man at a banquet. Equally hungry, she cuffed his wrists, rose on tiptoe and claimed him even as he branded her.

"Baby," he murmured, scattering kisses over her chin and jaw. He returned to her mouth and groaning, plunged deep, his tongue sweeping the interior.

Gwendolyn loosed his wrists and squeezed her arms between his to wrap him in a tight embrace. She clung to him, pressing her breasts to his hard chest. The rigid column of his erection nudged the flesh between her thighs and she rolled her hips against it, a sweet ache radiating from her sex to every limb.

She dragged her mouth away from his.

"Xavier." Her breath burst from her lungs as she buried her face in the crook between his neck and shoulder.

"Why didn't you tell me, baby?" He released her face, but as if he couldn't bear to stop touching her, he cupped her nape and gripped her waist.

She lifted her head and shook it. "I thought you would blame me for his death. I did."

"What are you talking about?"

"Josh was so angry that night." The images were so clear even six years later. "I couldn't blame him. I'd hurt him so horribly and I hated myself for a long time. When he left, he wasn't rational. If I hadn't ended the engagement, he wouldn't have been so upset. He wouldn't have died."

Finally, she'd admitted her secret guilt. Silence permeated the room. Each second ticking by was like a lifetime and she couldn't bear not knowing his reaction. She opened her eyes.

And stared into the face of redemption.

A soft cry escaped her lips. She bowed her head and leaned forward until her forehead bumped his chin.

"I was so scared," she rasped, voice hoarse with the weight of unshed tears. "So scared you would hold me responsible."

"Gwen. Baby." Xavier pinched her chin and tilted her head back, forcing her to look at him. "Joshua's accident was a senseless tragedy. No one is to blame. For six years you've been a prisoner of a shame not belonging to you. If you had come to me, I would have never let you bear the burden alone."

Again she shook her head. "That would have been incredibly unfair. You were with Evelyn and dealing with your younger brother's death. How could I tell you I had broken up with Josh the night before our wedding because I loved you?"

"How could you not?"

The quiet question arrested her. Set her pulse off in rapid beats. Doubt veered toward longing. Longing edged toward cautious joy.

"Your turn," she insisted and delivered the same demand he'd issued minutes earlier. "Tell me."

"I love you." Xavier speared his fingers through her curls, gripped her head tight and demanded her undivided attention. "I loved you when I had no right. Even when I felt guilty as hell for wanting you, I did." He gave her head a small shake. "You've pulled me back from the abyss, Gwen. I have hope when a week ago I was hopeless. I look into your eyes and believe I can be the man I once was. And the person I could be for you. With you."

"I've dreamed of you saying this to me." She touched his jaw, his lips, the precious, precious scar. "I never thought my dreams would come true."

Xavier lowered his head and brushed a kiss over her mouth. Joy filled her, spilled over in breathless laughter.

"I love you," she vowed and reached up to cradle his cheek. "So, where do we go from here?"

A blinding smile spread wide over his face, stunning in its beauty.

"Why that's simple, baby," he murmured, and she melted at the tenderness reflected in his eyes. "We live happily ever after."

A PERFECT FIT

For no-nonsense, less-than-warm Rowyn Jeong, being labeled the plainer, wicked stepsister has never bothered her...until Darius Fiore reappears in her life. Months ago, they indulged in a hot one-night stand, and the sexy business tycoon branded her like no man had before. But his return threatens her position within her stepfather's company, and he's the man her stepsister Cindy has within her sights—and hands.

Behind closed doors, Daruis discovered more lay beneath Rowyn's hard exterior than the ice queen she presents to her family. Now, he understands the aloof reserve. Her family's disregard has left her hungry for love and acceptance. But breaking down her walls will be no easy task. Especially since his presence threatens everything she's worked so hard to achieve.

Author Note

The *Cinderella* quotes found at the beginning of each chapter are from the work of seventeenth century French author Charles Perrault, as well as eighteenth century fairytale collectors the Brothers Grimm. No mice, pumpkins or footmen were injured in the retelling.

CHAPTER ONE

"...and without a word of good-bye, she slipped from the prince's arms and ran down the steps. As she ran, she lost one of her slippers..."—Cinderella

"Son of a bitch! Where is it?"—Rowyn Jeong

"No, open your eyes." A big hand smoothed her damp, tangled hair from her face. The backs of his long fingers grazed her cheek. "I want you to see."

Her breath shuddered from between her parted lips, and after the slightest hesitation she complied with his soft command. She lifted her lashes and the erotic tableau that met her eyes stole the air from her lungs. *Oh God.*

The deep shadows reflected in the bureau mirror couldn't hide the long arch of a masculine back, the curve of a taut buttock or the muscled length of thigh. So much sexuality contained under golden skin. The perfect male animal.

Her pussy clenched.

"That's it, baby," he murmured in her ear. "Squeeze me tight."

His ass rose and the drag of his cock pulsed through her swollen sex as his thick, gleaming shaft withdrew from her body. Restrained underneath him by his chest and hands, she could do nothing but gasp and receive the pleasure he seemed intent on giving over and over. It wasn't the first or even the second time she'd been pinned and penetrated this night. But as the incredible length of his dick tunneled through her pussy once more, it may as well have been the first. Her flesh resisted, parted, gripped. Every inch, every ridge seemed to imprint a fiery brand on her sex.

He groaned and in a fraction of a second, he tightened his fingers on her wrists. With him stretched over her, his chest pressing into her spine, the shiver that coursed through his big body vibrated over her skin like an electrical charge.

Once more he slid free. She shuddered.

"Do you have any idea how much my cock wants your pussy?" he whispered. He straightened and hooked an arm under her hips, pulled her ass up and back. He followed the line of her spine, sliding a palm over the ball of her shoulder and then down again. "There, baby. Watch it. Watch my dick take you." The pale column of flesh speared from a thatch of brown hair and arrowed straight between her trembling thighs. His cock disappeared from sight as it surged deep in her sex. Her stomach muscles quivered and she sank her teeth into her bottom lip at the erotic image. It seemed naughty, forbidden, to watch herself getting fucked. But damn—another groan ripped free from his throat as he fisted his cock near the flared base—she couldn't turn away from the mirror's reflection. "Your pussy's so fucking drenched. Like hot cream. Like you're melting around my dick…"

The dual stimulation of his sexy words and witnessing her own fucking pushed her so close to orgasm she shook under the whip of lust. Tiny flicks of pleasure lashed her clit and her pussy rippled around his thick cock. She wanted to *come*.

As if sensing her heightened need, he surged forward. He buried his length inside her, his thighs pressed tight to her legs and the lower curves of her ass. Pleasure tore a cry from her throat and she bucked helplessly against the hard thrust.

"Good girl," he praised. "Fuck my cock, pretty girl." He fell forward, palms flat against the dark mahogany headboard. It didn't seem possible he had more cock to give her, but *God*, when he pushed deeper into her pussy, he nudged a place high in her sex that'd never been touched by human or mechanical means. He grunted and his hips pressed forward, grinding against her ass. He slid one hand between her thighs and plucked her clit.

She screamed.

Her response seemed to snap the binding that tethered his control. With a low animalistic growl, he fucked her like a stallion covering his mare. He rode her hard, slamming into her with thrust after thrust. She cried out with each stroke, urging him on, begging for more. God. *More.*

The orgasm pummeled her like a battering ram. No slow buildup, no undulation of pleasure to signal its arrival. Just a crash of ecstasy. A shattering of self.

Then nothing.

Oh. Shit.

* * * * *

Rowyn Jeong cast a glance down her body to the heavy arm roped across her waist. Her heart thumped. The shallow gasps of breath that escaped her lips seemed unnaturally loud in the quiet room as her gaze skipped up an arm, over a shoulder and landed on a long expanse of delectable skin.

Jesus. She sighed and then cringed as her breath seemed to echo in the room like a shout across the Grand Canyon. Muscles tense, she lay frozen as if she were engaged in some twisted erotic version of Red Light, Green Light. For several long moments she remained still, her gaze pinned on the naked man next to her, searching for any sign of wakefulness. After seconds that stretched like a millennium, she inched from under the arm.

Scoot. Pause. Breathe. Scoot. Pause. Breathe. She repeated the pattern until her arm, hip, then leg dangled over the edge of the mattress like limp spaghetti. One more scoot and she slid free. Unable to halt her momentum, she flailed and her ass hit the floor with a thump.

Damn.

She shut her eyes and dropped her chin.

Just Damn.

She risked a peek over the side of the bed and her inspection took in the still form. His arm stretched across the snowy sheet. His chest continued to rise and fall, undisturbed. She didn't look away as she edged back from the bed, the man in it, and memories of the night that had just passed. A hot flash of heat licked over her skin and the swollen, well-used flesh between her thighs rippled.

She had to get out of here. Like, pronto.

In a hushed flurry of activity, Rowyn jumped to her feet and circled the room, snatching up clothing that had been hastily discarded earlier in the evening. Panties in her fist—how the hell had they ended up hanging from the lamp shade?—she scurried from the dark room. With a speed that smacked more of desperation than skill, she yanked on her underwear followed by the black sweater and skirt.

On bare feet, she darted down the shadowed hall and into the living room. Minutes later, a taxi had been requested on her cell phone, her purse was over her shoulder and her boots and coat had been dragged on. As she headed toward the front door, she passed the hall mirror and glimpsed her reflection. She skidded to a halt. *Shit.* She looked as if she'd just spent the night fucking.

With a moue of disgust, she tunneled her fingers through her dark hair and tried to comb some semblance of order into it so she wouldn't look so freshly fucked. After several fruitless moments, she gritted her teeth. *To hell with it.* She scowled and shoved the heavy strands back over her shoulder. She couldn't do anything about...

Her eyes narrowed and then widened in horror as she stared at her neck—her bare neck. The delicate gold chain and pendant with a tiny crown etched into its surface were gone. *To my princess.* The jewelry and loving message engraved in Korean on the back of the ornament were the only legacy she had from her dead father besides her almond-shaped eyes and nearly black, dense hair.

Dammit! She dropped her hands, whipped around and dashed back down the hall, the spiky heels of her stiletto boots clacking out an agitated cadence on the hardwood floor. *Where is it?* She conducted a circuit of the living room, jerking pillows and cushions off the couch and love seat and ghosting her palm over the glass surface of the coffee table. Finally, after long frustrating minutes with her heart lodged in her throat, she stood in the middle of the room, one hand cupping her forehead and the other resting on her collarbone. She was naked—bereft without the jewelry. She couldn't leave—

A short toot of a horn beeped outside. The taxi had arrived.

With one last desperate glance down the darkened hall, she turned and retraced her steps toward the front door...leaving a part of her heart behind...

CHAPTER TWO

"Once upon a time, there was a widower who married a proud and haughty woman as his second wife... By his first wife he'd had a beautiful daughter, who was a girl of unparalleled goodness and sweet temper."—Cinderella

"Nobody's that damn nice."—Rowyn Jeong

"New assistant not working out?"

Rowyn glanced up from her computer and met the dark-brown gaze of her coworker and friend Wanda Dixon.

"Hmm?" she asked, returning her attention to the report on her monitor. A surge of satisfaction rose up in her chest as she studied the budget. The second quarter numbers were right on target. She shifted her gaze from the quarterly financial statement as Wanda entered the office and closed the door behind her. "What did you say?"

Wanda shook her head and crossed the room. As she sank onto the chair in front of the desk, the elegant fit of her lilac wraparound dress caught Rowyn's eye. The soft color complimented the woman's smooth, brown skin and the silk glided over her tall, lithe body. Rowyn tapped a fingertip against her lip. That style might be just the thing they needed to complete the fall collection for the store...

"I said, the new assistant must not be working out."

Rowyn frowned as she picked up a pen and jotted down a note about looking into that dress. "What are you talking about?"

"I just passed by your secretary of one week, her purse over her shoulder and a cardboard box under one arm." Wanda arched an eyebrow. "Crying."

"What the hell?" Rowyn demanded. "Did she say anything?"

"Yeah." The other woman snorted. "'That bitch is crazy.'"

"Funny," Rowyn drawled. She dropped her pen on the desk and fell back in her chair, irritated. "Well, damn. This is an inconvenient time to quit. She could've at least waited until the end of the day. I have a conference call at three and I needed her to take notes." She reached for the phone. "You think Human Resources will send up a temporary replacement?"

"Doubtful." Wanda smirked. "After three—well four, counting the one that just left—different assistants in seven months, you've earned a bit of a reputation."

"Reputation, my ass," Rowyn growled and jabbed a finger in the air toward Wanda. "All I asked her to do was rewrite a report and use fucking spell-check and a dictionary next time. Excuse me if I offended her tender sensibilities." She sneered. "I'm not a total bitch—"

"Partial maybe, but definitely not total," Wanda agreed. It's not my fault that the last three—"

"Four, actually."

"Assistants couldn't stick around and grow some balls," Rowyn concluded with a glare.

Unperturbed, Wanda held up her hand, stretched her fingers wide and pretended to study her immaculate manicure. "Maybe they could borrow a couple from you. From what I hear, you have a very nice brass pair." When Rowyn flipped her off Wanda's peal of laughter rang throughout the office. "Very eloquent comeback, my friend." She chuckled then slipped one slim leg over the other, rested an elbow on her knee and settled her chin in her palm. "As much as I enjoy commiserating over your employee— or lack of employee— issues, that isn't why I came by. I have tickets to the Maroon 5 concert tonight. And great friend that I am, thought of you. So how 'bout it? Want to go?"

"You're kidding!" Her voice rose several octaves and she didn't care that she sounded like a teenager screeching over her favorite rock band. Excitement swept Rowyn's annoyance aside like a tornado winding through an Alabama trailer park.

Hell, given the chance, she would throw Bret Michaels *her* panties. "Of course I want— Oh damn. Damn. Damn." She slapped the heel of her palm against her forehead, punctuating each "damn" with a thump. "I can't."

Wanda's eyes widened and her arm fell across her knee as she leaned forward. "You can't go see your favorite eighties hair band? Is there a world summit on global peace I'm not aware of?"

Rowyn snorted. "Not likely. Daniel invited a potential business associate over for dinner. And Mom demanded my presence for a performance of the Harrison version of the Partridge Family." She smiled grimly. "Tonight's showing begins at 8:00 p.m. and I am slotted to play the role of adoring older daughter."

"Oh God." Wanda shuddered. "You'd turn down Poison to attend the dinner from hell?"

Rowyn shook her head and winced as thoughts of spending the evening with her stepfather, mother and stepsister flitted through her mind like a horror movie.

"Believe me," she said, "if I could avoid this, I would. But it's either go and endure torture for a couple of hours or not go and endure Mom's diatribe about what an ungrateful, inconsiderate daughter I am for the next couple of months."

"Well, when you put it like that," her friend conceded. "My condolences."

"I need them." Rowyn squeezed her forehead between her thumb and middle finger. "It's going to be one hell of a night."

8:15 p.m. Shit. She was late.

* * * * *

The Harrisons' long-time housekeeper Margaret opened the front door at Rowyn's knock. When the older woman smiled and stepped back for her to pass, it occurred to Rowyn the housekeeper might be the only person pleased to see her tonight. Her mother Pamela Wright Harrison would be pissed because she'd arrived late. Daniel Harrison, her mother's second husband and Rowyn's stepfather, would be irritated because of the interruption her arrival would cause. And her stepsister Cynthia—or Cindy as they all called her—would wear her usual pretty smile and add a vapid comment or two.

Fun, fun, fun.

Yeah. Like a stake in the eye.

"They are in the small living room," Margaret said, taking Rowyn's purse.

"Thanks, Maggie." Rowyn inhaled and released the breath in a low gust of air. She stretched her lips into the brightest, phoniest smile she could manage. "Here's my social smile," she murmured through clenched teeth and a stiff mouth. "How does it look?"

Margaret chuckled and shook her head. "Lovely, Ms. Rowyn."

The older woman turned and headed toward the hall closet, still laughing softly. Rowyn stared after her. The hair contained more gray strands now than black. The drill sergeant stride that had struck awe and fear in Rowyn's heart as a child had slowed a bit. It dawned on her like the coming of a new day that if this proud woman were gone, Rowyn would lose the only person who had loved her unconditionally.

She'd entered this home at her mother's side a scared and nervous eleven-year-old, trying so hard to mimic Pamela's aloof expression. But Maggie had taken one look at her and detected the fear lurking beneath the adult mask. And through the years the housekeeper had loved Rowyn—even when she'd been unlovable.

Amusement mingled with the pang of sadness. And there were certainly times when she'd been damn unlovable.

As she turned toward the living room entrance, her humor drained away like the alcohol which doubtless flowed too easily down her mother's throat. With her hand on the knob, Rowyn slabbed layer after layer of mental cement around her emotions and heart. A quick scan ensured no cracks existed and she twisted the knob, pushed open the door and entered.

And walked into Charlotte Bronte's version of hell.

Daniel faced the entrance, speaking animatedly to the tall man across from him. Her mother—surprise, surprise, with a highball raised to her lips—and stepsister filled in the small circle. At the snick of the door closing behind Rowyn, all four turned to stare in her direction.

Oh. Damn.

The gasp remained trapped in her throat and the world screeched to a halt as if God had slammed his foot on the brakes of time. She sucked in a breath—a difficult task since all the air seemed to have been vacuumed out of the room. Perspiration prickled her palms and if she could have moved, she would have rubbed them against her skirt.

It can't be. She stared, her heart performing a dizzying tap dance against her rib cage. *It's not possible.*

Yet meeting the bright blue eyes that had haunted her dreams for the past six months, Rowyn couldn't deny what her gaze refused to accept.

Him.

She'd convinced herself he couldn't possibly have been as beautiful in reality as he'd appeared in her dreams. After all, when a man gave a woman the most intense, just-this-side-of-death orgasms she'd ever experienced, she could be forgiven for imagining him larger than life. But no, as he stood mere feet away, staring at her with his impenetrable gaze, Rowyn realized her dreams hadn't been exaggerations.

The same deep cobalt eyes that reminded her of the heart of the ocean. The same olive-tinted skin that reminded her of Italian villas perched on craggy cliffs and romantic beaches. The same beauty that, if he'd been born centuries earlier, would have had Michelangelo drooling to sculpt him for his *David*. His dark-brown, closely-cropped curls enhanced the image of a Greco-Roman work of art. And Jesus, the body...She shivered. Tall, elegant and hinting at the almost-primitive power that existed under the civilized black jacket, slacks and maroon shirt.

She'd been on the receiving end of that power, unleashed and wild.

The intense stare held her immobile and might as well have been a length of steel chains wrapped around her body. She couldn't move, couldn't avoid the hard questions in his penetrating gaze.

Unbidden, the memory of the last time she'd been with him flared in her mind. Just the thought of that night made her nipples tingle and her sex clench. There were nights she still woke from erotic, Technicolor dreams, body trembling and breath rasping out of her throat. Dreams of a face hardened with lust, gleaming blue eyes and a big, muscled body sliding on top of hers, his cock thrusting deep in her pussy. Stretching and filling her...

Rowyn glanced away. Damn. All this time later and an emptiness still lingered—a hollow emptiness that could only be filled by a man she believed she'd never see again...the man not five feet away.

"Rowyn," Pamela drawled, snatching her from the stupor she'd tumbled into. "How nice of you to show up. Late."

The barb might as well have been a rubber ball for it bounced right off Rowyn.

What was Darius doing here? In Boston?

"Darius, please forgive my daughter. She's a terrible workaholic." Her mother's smile was nothing but a tight pull of her lips. "Gets that from her father, I'm afraid."

Rowyn gritted her teeth. The other people in the room may have assumed Pamela referred to Daniel Harrison, but her mother meant Rowyn's biological father Charles Jeong. The man Pamela resented even eight years after his death.

"I apologize." Rowyn finally found her voice.

Daniel stepped forward. "Darius, I'd like to introduce my stepdaughter, Rowyn Jeong. Rowyn," he nodded toward the man who'd stepped straight from her most erotic dreams, "this is Darius Fiore, a business associate from Seattle."

"Nice to meet you." Her greeting sounded formal, polite, and as if she'd never sucked his cock to the back of her throat.

A small half-smile tipped a corner of Darius' mouth and, for a moment, she feared he would mention they knew one another—biblically. But no. He stepped forward and extended his hand. "It's a pleasure, Ms. Jeong."

Rowyn accepted his hand and he closed his fingers around hers and squeezed. She stared down at their clasped hands and was pummeled by flashes of those same long, elegant fingers stroking in and out of her pursed lips as he demonstrated how he wanted her to suck his cock. Her clit set up a pounding like the drum section in a marching band. Cream moistened her slit and *God*, she swore that even now, months later, the tangy flavor of his skin lingered on her tongue.

Her breath rasped in her throat and she snatched her hand away as if his palm held a live coal. She avoided his gaze and shifted back a couple steps, placing distance between them. So close to him, his fresh-air-and-sunbaked-sand scent enveloped her and she imagined him holding her against his body, his arms wrapped around her. She withdrew another step.

"Are you okay?" he murmured, reaching out to steady her.

"Yes, fine," she stammered and moved her arm out of his reach. She locked eyes with him again. "I'm fine."

"Rowyn is one of the most capable women I know." Cindy's

sweet bell-like voice interrupted their visual "noon showdown". Her younger, gorgeous stepsister slipped an arm through Darius' and offered Rowyn a glass of wine. "If she claims she's okay then believe me, she is." She chuckled, the pure tinkle of laughter as delightful as everything else about her sister, and guided Darius back to Daniel and Pamela, leaving Rowyn to follow.

Rowyn contemplated the pair. Objectively they made a striking couple. Cindy's brown curls brushed his shoulder, making his tall stature appear even more so, her slender frame the perfect foil for his strong, broad-shouldered physique.

But subjectively, Rowyn wanted to warn Cindy that if she didn't remove her touch from Darius, she'd draw back a nub.

Jesus. This is going to be a long-ass evening.

"I've always wanted to visit Seattle," Cindy commented, smiling up at Darius. "It's beautiful scenery. So picturesque and romantic." She cast a glance over her shoulder in Rowyn's direction. "Rowyn has been there several times, though. On business, of course."

"What other reason would she have to travel? Our Rowyn is married to her job." Pamela's brittle laugh failed to blunt the verbal slice. After thirty years of emotional stabs, Rowyn should have ceased to bleed fifteen years ago.

"It is a beautiful part of the country," Darius said, smoothly filling the uncomfortable silence following Pamela's thinly veiled barb. "I moved there ten years ago from Florida and I've never regretted it."

"I'm sure Seattle has never regretted it either," Daniel said, clapping the younger man on the shoulder. "The employment rate must have had a boost with your chain of department stores."

Rowyn fought to contain her surprise. It had never occurred to her that she and Darius worked in the same field. Of course, they hadn't talked about business that night. Funny how she knew his favorite movie was *The Breakfast Club*, he had no clue who Lady Gaga was and he couldn't pass by a Hershey bar with almonds without buying one. But how he earned his living had never surfaced in their myriad conversation topics.

Then again, maybe not so funny. That night she had craved being someone other than Rowyn the coldhearted businesswoman. Rowyn the plainer, bitchier stepsister.

Rowyn the out-of-wedlock mistake.

She studied the dark-red depths of her glass, imagining it were a crystal ball. Maybe this explained why her mother drank like a fish. Maybe she too hoped answers lay at the bottom of her glass.

"With the success and popularity of your women's department, this merger could be highly profitable for both of us."

Merger? Rowyn frowned and fixed her gaze and attention on Daniel. She hadn't heard the slightest whisper of a joint venture with another company.

"You're considering merging, Daniel?" she asked, voice as placid as she could manage even though disquiet rippled through her stomach.

"Yes." Her stepfather regarded her with a faintly puzzled frown. *Maybe he forgot I'm still standing here.* "We're discussing the possibility of starting off small. Just the women's fashion department for now."

The quivers swelled into breakers that threatened to tow her under their water of disbelief, anger...and hurt. After years of Daniel's indifference and careless, sporadic affection, Rowyn had believed her stepfather could no longer hurt her. *I stand corrected.*

"Since that is my division, what would happen to the offices here? As well as the employees?" *Me?*

A furrow of irritation appeared between his brows as if her questions were too pesky to address...as if his stepdaughter was too inconsequential to consider.

"All that can be worked out." He waved off her concerns with a small flick of his hand. "Everyone can be reassigned."

The pain radiated out from the center of her chest and infected every part of her body until Rowyn throbbed like a walking wound.

Everyone.

She'd busted her ass for his company—for *him*—for five years. The long hours, the hard work...They were all she had to offer Daniel that he would willingly take. Never had Rowyn disillusioned herself that she could win his love—that had been reserved for his dead first wife and their daughter—so she'd given him the one thing she had. And now he'd literally brushed her dedication off as one would an annoying gnat.

Jesus. When would she learn?

When the hell would she stop caring?

CHAPTER THREE

"When the prince set eyes on Cinderella, he was struck by her beauty. Walking over to her, he bowed deeply and asked her to dance. And to the great disappointment of all the young ladies, he danced with Cinderella all evening."—Cinderella

"Welcome back, buddy."—Darius Fiore to his penis after seeing Rowyn Jeong again.

When Darius turned twelve, his cousin Jared liberated the new four-wheeler he'd received for his birthday and wrecked it before Darius had a chance to ride it. At twenty, he caught the college undergraduate he believed himself in love with treating her economics professor to a late-night blow job. She thought Darius should have understood—since she needed a C—as the class was in her major.

And at twenty-five, his father had promoted a lazy imbecile over him because he hadn't wanted his son to rise too quickly in the family business. That same month, he divorced Darius' mother and married the aforementioned undergraduate. Apparently the economics professor wasn't the only man she'd been blowing behind Darius' back.

In every one of those experiences, Darius had been mad as hell. But not one compared to the fury that consumed him as he stood next to Daniel Harrison and witnessed the disregard and cold rejection he inflicted on his oldest daughter. Correction—*stepdaughter*, as the businessman had been quick to point out when Darius had inquired about her.

Blood relation or not, she deserved more respect than Daniel had granted. Before considering partnering up with Harrison Companies, Darius had researched the huge chain. Numbers didn't lie. The business' main income was derived from the women's fashion division. And its success could be directly attributed to Rowyn Jeong.

Of course when he'd read her name on his reports, he hadn't realized the departmental head and the woman he'd nearly killed himself fucking six months ago were one and the same.

He paused inside the entrance to the living room they'd congregated in earlier. She stood at one of the long oblong windows, staring out into the darkness. For the moment they had the room to themselves. Her parents had been held up by their housekeeper and Cindy had excused herself, most likely too polite to say she needed to go to the bathroom.

As he stared at the proud line of Rowyn's spine in the simple but stylish wine-red sheath, Darius was thankful for the time to study her. Ramrod straight. Unbending. A perfect description of the woman he'd spent the evening facing across the dinner table. With a reserve that rode the edge of detachment, Rowyn had dined quietly while her stepfather alternated between boasting about his company and rhapsodizing his younger daughter's virtues, her mother complained and emptied glass after glass of wine and her stepsister chattered nonstop about...hell, whatever. He'd stopped listening after the first mind-numbing round of local gossip.

Through the long dinner hour, Rowyn had appeared untouched, even indifferent. Yet he'd spied the flicker of hurt that had darkened her eyes at Daniel's callous rebuff. And he'd detected the minute cracks in her armor as Pamela delivered well-aimed jabs and cutting remarks.

For an educated woman, you have nothing relevant to add to this conversation. I wish you would do something with your hair. No wonder a man isn't attracted to you.

Jesus. It almost seemed as if she *disliked* her daughter. He had wanted to jump in and demand the older woman lay the fuck off. He'd wanted to catch Rowyn's gaze, assure her she wasn't alone in this battle that masqueraded as dinner. But Rowyn had studiously avoided making eye contact with him, and he'd had to swallow his disappointment along with the Sir Galahad syndrome that had reared its chivalrous head.

He could have saved his worry, though. Rowyn had taken her mother's verbal stabs in stride. If he hadn't been studying her so closely, he would have missed the slight tightening of her lips and the small tilt of her chin.

Who *was* Rowyn Jeong? The contained, aloof businesswoman? Or the sensual, uninhibited lover who had disappeared without a hint to her existence except for the lingering scent of sex on his bed sheets and a beautiful necklace and pendant.

Determined to find out, Darius stepped forward. Her back stiffened as he approached, but she didn't turn to face him. He didn't pause until the lapel of his jacket grazed the deep-red satin of her dress.

He shoved his hands in the pockets of his slacks. It was either that or grab her arms, turn her around and lick the curve of her plump bottom lip before sliding his tongue deep into the mouth he'd had wet dreams about.

Their eyes met and held for a brief space of time in the darkened window that reflected their images. Unlike Cindy, the top of Rowyn's head grazed his chin and he didn't feel like a hulking giant next to Thumbelina. From experience, he knew her sexy curves complimented his body like the perfect puzzle piece. Again and again her breasts had pressed to his chest, his hips to that beautiful rounded ass. He inhaled. And like a deer scenting water, his body reacted to her skin's perfume.

His breathing deepened. His skin prickled. His cock hardened to the point of sweet pain. Fuck, the smell of her was like a hot palm squeezing his dick.

"Did you just smell my hair?"

The husky tone contradicted the sharp words. Her back remained to him, but Darius glimpsed the narrowing of her eyes in the window.

"Yes, I think I did." From her silence, he assumed his candor surprised her. He could have lied. Probably should have. But considering the lurid images that had been running through his mind from the moment she'd walked through that living room door over an hour ago, smelling her hair seemed pretty low on the you're-a-sick-fuck list. Hell, every time she'd closed her lips around her fork, he'd pictured Rowyn as she'd been that night—kneeling before him, her pretty mouth stretched wide around his cock, her moans vibrating along his skin, dark eyes gleaming with pleasure…

His skin was tight as shit—a dry-clean-only suit that had been washed. His cock throbbed and lust gripped his gut in a headlock. In six months, no other woman had made his dick twitch much less harden to a full erection. Shit, if not for the fact it jerked and erupted in his hand every night to thoughts of this woman, he would've believed an emergency regimen of Viagra was in order.

Rowyn turned to face him. Without flinching, she tilted her head back to meet his stare. No fidgeting. No hint of coyness. No flirting. And damn, wasn't that hot?

"At the risk of sounding cliché, it's a very small world," Darius murmured. The understatement of the century.

"Somehow I don't believe Walt Disney meant encountering someone he'd seen naked. Or in his parents' home," Rowyn drawled.

Though the image of a tuxedo-clothed cricket bumping uglies was disturbing, he couldn't suppress the spurt of humor at her dry wit. It had been one of the characteristics that had captured his attention and kept him pinned to that barstool all those months ago. It was also one that had failed to make an appearance this evening until now. And now, as then, it only enhanced the natural beauty and allure that even her cool demeanor, restrained hair and subtle clothing couldn't hide.

"No wonder I couldn't find you," he said, shifting closer, trespassing her space. This close, he didn't miss the glint of irritation that flickered in her eyes. Oh yeah, this woman would guard her personal territory and obviously resented his invasion. But she didn't back up either. He'd known her straightforward manner was hot…but damn, make that hot as fuck.

Unable to stop himself, he lifted a hand to her face and stroked his thumb over the lush bottom lip that fascinated him. He wanted to bite it, suck the sweet flesh between his teeth. His dick jerked, totally on board with the idea.

"Did you know there are fifty-six 'Rowyns' in the greater Seattle area?" he asked softly.

"You searched for me?"

Darius ignored her question and the disbelief that coated it. In one motion, he dropped his hand and retreated away from temptation. Need seemed to replace the air in his lungs, the blood in his veins. The exotic almond shape of her heavily lashed eyes, the high, aristocratic cheekbones, the sinful mouth… He stifled a groan and retreated another step. God should have made her the eleventh commandment.

"Why did you leave?" The words seemed to erupt from his lips. The question had plagued him since that night and couldn't be contained a moment longer. Had he demanded too much from her? Had he hurt her in some way?

The worry had been like an insistent itch at the back of his neck that he couldn't ease. His memories were of a hot night filled with the most incredible sex with an equally incredible woman. As he'd fallen asleep, waking up to that same woman and learning more about her had been his last coherent thought.

Instead he'd woken to an empty bed and an emptier hole in his gut, as if he'd been offered the opportunity to partake of a sumptuous feast and had arrived too late.

Rowyn blinked then cocked her head, her expression as bland as her tone. "To stay two nights would have been a bit counterproductive to the purpose of a one-night stand."

He arched an eyebrow. Since he was fourteen, women had cozied up to him, flirted—as much for his appearance as well as his father's money.

None had wham-bam-thank-you-ma'amed him.

"You know," he drawled and reclaimed the distance he'd placed between them, "if I hadn't seen you mid-orgasm, I might buy this freeze-ice-cubes-on-your-ass routine." He touched her again. This time right where her stomach and pelvic region merged. He dropped his gaze. If she were naked, he'd probably graze the top of that neatly trimmed nest of black hair covering her pussy. He heard the loud intake of breath and her abdominal muscles clenched, going concave beneath his fingers. "Now that sound I clearly remember. Every time I pushed my cock into your tight pussy you'd suck in a breath and hold it."

He sketched a small circle over her dress, applying enough pressure her soft flesh gave beneath his fingers. "Remember the first time I fucked you? God, it took forever for your pussy to loosen around my dick. I had to move *so* slow. It was torture feeling those muscles quiver around me. I almost lost it before I was fully inside. You were so wet, so small."

He groaned and widened the circle, coming perilously close to the top of her sex. The rasp of air from Rowyn's lungs confirmed his assumption—heat burned beneath the ice queen facade. "But the second time you took me easier. And the third..." He glanced up and beheld eyes that were anything but cold. They gleamed with heat. Her lush lips parted under her pants and a delicate flush colored her high cheekbones. Fuck, she was beautiful. "The third time," he breathed, "I slid right in as if I'd broken in your pussy with my cock."

A small, inarticulate cry escaped her and she shuddered. Thick lashes lowered. "Sweetheart," he murmured and slid a finger lower.

"There you two are," a cheery voice interrupted, shattering the desire-thickened tension woven around them like a cocoon.

In an instant, the passion of a woman on the verge of surrender gave way to such stricken vulnerability Darius bit off a blistering curse. He turned around and blocked Rowyn from her sister's view. Even as he faced Cindy and forced a stiff smile to his lips, nothing could erase that haunted expression from his mind.

"Dad wanted to give you a tour of the house, Darius." Cindy crossed the room and linked an arm through his. She tipped her head back then gave him a pretty grin and flirtatious squeeze. "He'd like to show you where the party will be held Saturday night. You are staying in town for it, aren't you?" She guided him toward the opened door of the room and he allowed it. As he responded to her question about his plans, his thoughts lingered on the silent woman who remained in the living room.

No doubt shoring up her prickly defenses. Good thing he didn't mind getting scratched.

CHAPTER FOUR

"When another ball was held the next evening, Cinderella again attended with her Godmother's help. The prince became even more entranced."—Cinderella

"What? Do I have broccoli stuck between my teeth?"—Rowyn Jeong

"I'm coming!"

Rowyn almost flew down the staircase, shoving pins in her chignon as she hurried to answer the insistent ringing of her doorbell. A harried glance at her wristwatch revealed the time—7:30 a.m. A barrage of thoughts raced through her mind and set her heart pounding. Her mother. Cindy. An accident. It had to be bad news to bring someone to her door, much less this early in the morning.

God, please let them be all right...

She gripped the knob with one hand and twisted the lock with the other. Not bothering to peek out the side window, Rowyn jerked the door open.

And stared.

"Good morning." Darius grinned down at her. What. The. Fuck.

"Please tell me you're bringing news of a tragic car accident and have beaten the police to my door."

He arched a dark eyebrow. Rather than respond, he held out a Styrofoam cup. A thin wisp of vapor rose from its lid, bringing with it the seductive aroma of freshly brewed coffee. She scowled and folded her arms across her chest. He didn't really think he could distract her with coffee, did he?

Darius sighed. "No tragic accident. Why would you think that?"

"It is the only explanation for your showing up at my house this early in the morning. Hell, showing up at my house—period," she snapped.

"Such a gracious host." He tsked, shaking his head, a small smile playing about his full lips. Damn, those lips. The things he could do with them... She delivered a mental slap to herself with a sharp order to get it together. But the warning came too late. He had already maneuvered his way past her and into the foyer of her home.

With a low growl of irritation, Rowyn slammed the door behind him. Darius turned and once again, she ignored the offer of the cup.

"What are you doing here?" Jesus, she shrieked like a shrew. And yet she couldn't stop the anxiety that sharpened her voice. Her home was her domain. Her sanctuary. The four years she'd lived in the Back Bay house, no one but Wanda had been allowed inside.

Without glancing behind her, she knew the soft colors, overstuffed couches and landscape paintings he studied represented a side of her she didn't reveal to many people. His survey of the airy living room that opened off the small foyer caused a vulnerability she detested.

"Very nice," he commented, bringing his inspection to rest on her face. With those deep blue eyes that seemed to see far too much, the touch of his gaze was almost tactile. She resisted rubbing her face to discover if she'd inadvertently left behind a dab of moisturizer.

"What?" she asked, wheezing as if she'd just sprinted around the block.

"Nothing," he said and, with the same half-smile quirking a corner of his mouth, extended the coffee cup again. "Please," he murmured.

"Shit," she mumbled and accepted the hot drink. Their fingertips brushed and a bolt of lightning charged up her arm, straight to her breasts and zinged to her pussy. Winded, she glanced down at her linen sheath, amazed no scorch patterns appeared on her clothes. She flicked her eyes up and slammed into such heat, the raw power in his gaze intensified the sweet ache in her nipples and between her thighs.

God, his stare seemed to burn a hole right through her.

Had anyone ever looked at her like that before? Yes. He had. While stripping her clothes from her body. While staring up at her from between her spread thighs as he circled her clit with his tongue in a wicked caress. While pounding into her pussy with such force the headboard had banged against the wall in time to his measured and deliberate thrusts.

Blood rushed between her thighs, and even now the echo of those demanding strokes pulsed deep in her sex. Moisture glazed her slit, drenching her panties. The power this man had over her body with one look. It should be criminal.

Rowyn ducked her head on the pretense of drinking her coffee and stepped back.

She lifted the cup to her mouth, sipped and jerked her head up in shock.

"You know how I take my coffee?" she asked, the creamy flavor of the brew still on her tongue. Most people would assume a ball-buster like her would prefer her coffee black, not liberally sweetened with cream and sugar.

"You ordered a cup before we left the bar," he reminded her and cocked his head, studying her. "There isn't much I don't remember about you, Rowyn."

Silence filled the foyer. His words dropped in her soul like a pebble in a pool of water and unfamiliar warmth rippled out in ever-widening rings of tenderness. He barely knew her and yet he'd noticed and remembered her likes. She couldn't even say the same about her family.

"Well..." She cleared her throat and curled her toes self-consciously against the cool wood floor. "What are you doing here?"

"Since this is my first time to your city, I thought I'd do the tourist thing." He gave her what he probably considered a charming smile. And damn him, it was. "I couldn't think of a better guide than you."

"What have you been smoking?" Flames rushed up her neck and singed her face as he grinned wide. She grimaced and wondered where the hell her much-lauded reserve had disappeared to.

Rowyn made it an art of hiding her emotions behind a wall of indifference. She'd learned long ago if she didn't give a reaction, people—Pamela—didn't derive as much pleasure from needling and provoking her. So how Darius managed to slip under her defenses and wreak hell so effortlessly boggled her mind. "It's a workday, in case you haven't noticed. And that's where I'm headed. To work."

"Take a day off."

"I don't take days off," she protested, balking.

He arched a brow and she ground her teeth together, surprised she didn't exhale powdered enamel. God, she was beginning to hate that eyebrow.

"There's a first time for everything," he replied calmly. "Not today there—"

Darius held up a finger and her mind blanked at the imperious gesture. She blinked. Then blinked again. "Did you..." she sputtered. "Did you just *hold up a finger on me*?" Her voice rose a decibel with each word, outrage and disbelief jacking the volume up to the no-the-hell-he-didn't level.

"You're yelling," he pointed out.

"Damn right," she snarled and stabbed a finger toward the front door. "You can go now."

"Oh, I intend to," Darius agreed and slid a hand in the front pocket of his black pants, the coffee he'd bought for himself in the other. Unfortunately the loose fit did nothing to detract from his narrow waist, the strength of his muscled thighs or the impressive bulge under the zippered panel. "As soon as you change, we'll leave."

Rowyn tightened her grip on the cup while fisting her other hand at her side. *Ten, nine, eight, seven...*

"Are you growling?" That fucking brow *again*? By God she was going to snatch it off his forehead!

"I. Am. Going. To. Work."

"Hmmm..." He lifted the insulated coffee cup to his mouth and studied her over the lid. He sipped the coffee, the muscles of his throat working. Even the man's Adam's apple was sexy. "I can spend this day with you or I could accept Daniel's lunch invitation, followed by a round of golf. Of course I don't play, but I'm sure we could find all *sorts* of fascinating topics to discuss..."

Rowyn had grown up with Pamela as a mother so she understood anger. But never had she experienced the primal urge to kill. Maim. Dismember.

"Blackmail is not attractive," she snapped.

"Ah." He tapped a finger against his bottom lip. "But is it effective?" Darius smiled and she suspected he didn't try to conceal the satisfaction in his expression or tone.

He'd won this round and they both knew it.

"I'll be right back." She shot him a glare of disgust, and then wheeled around to head back up the stairs, warm cup still clasped in her hand.

And they accused *her* of having brass balls.

* * * * *

"Admit it. You're having a good time."

Rowyn slanted a glance at the man walking beside her. The hot afternoon sun beamed down on the walking trail next to the Charles River, highlighting the lighter shades of brown in his hair. The dark curls were long enough to form a sexy cap around his well-shaped head, but short enough to emphasize his patrician features. In a nutshell, he looked like the gorgeous Roman emperor he most likely descended from.

But the impression didn't stop with his appearance. His commanding presence, confident tilt of his chin, long-legged stride—they all attested to a man accustomed to leading and inspiring others to follow. The man had established a clothing empire that dominated the northwest and western markets. That kind of success took a special kind of grit and determination—not to mention brilliance.

And to top it all off, he could fuck as if he'd invented it.

"C'mon, Rowyn." He tipped his half-eaten strawberry ice cream cone in her direction. "'Fess up. You're enjoying yourself. You took a day off work and the world market didn't crash, California didn't plummet into the sea and the earth's core didn't implode."

She scrunched her nose. "Fine. It hasn't sucked."

Darius laughed, the rumble low and earthy. She couldn't help but smile in return. The day *hadn't* stunk. She swept her tongue over the banana ice cream topping her sugar cone. It had been wonderful. Though Rowyn had been ready to wipe the floor with him earlier, her anger had soon given way to the secret thrill of being with him.

In the dark, hidden place that was accessible only after several glasses of wine, she owned up to a shameful delight that he'd taken the choice of spending the day with him out of her hands. He'd made her concede to the desire her heart hungered for but her head denied.

The thought would undoubtedly get her women's lib card revoked, but Darius overrode all rational decision making.

They'd spent hours visiting such tourist traps as Faneuil Hall Market Place, Fenway Park—she shuddered in revulsion—the Bull and Finch Pub, better known as the *Cheers* bar, as well as the many shops and stores along Newbury Street. Even though she'd lived in Boston all her life, it had been years since she'd taken the leisure time to explore and enjoy her hometown. Not only was she seeing the historical landmarks and colorful sights through Darius's eyes, but through her own as well.

Something else to thank him for.

"Thank you," Darius said as he studied the quaint shops, vendors and buildings edging the banks of the Charles River before bringing his gaze back to her. He lifted his arm and stroked his free hand down the long tail of hair brushing her shoulder blades. She fought to not close her eyes at the gentle caress. The small tug on her scalp reverberated in her belly. *God.* She was thankful she'd chosen the more casual ponytail over the professional chignon. "The most experienced tour guide couldn't have treated me to the day you have."

Rowyn shrugged and pleasure at his praise coursed through her like a slow-moving current. This time she didn't ignore the fluttering in her stomach—she'd stopped the futile exercise hours ago.

"Blackmail aside," she drawled, "I'm glad I came. I'd forgotten how beautiful and fun Boston could be." Memories overwhelmed her as if the lock containing them had been picked and the mental images sprang free. A steel band constricted her chest and Rowyn fought to drag air into her lungs. "The last time I walked this trail was with my father. We'd spent the day together celebrating my fifteenth birthday."

"Are you close?" Darius asked, popping the last bite of his cone in his mouth.

"Were," Rowyn corrected. And the pain throbbing in her heart vibrated in her voice. "He died eight years ago."

"Oh sweetheart," he murmured and reached toward her. His larger hand engulfed her smaller one and held tight. "I'm so sorry." He drew her closer and she didn't resist, needing his comforting nearness. "I didn't know."

"No." She shook her head. "It's okay. And to answer your question, no, we weren't very close. Before he died, we were trying to rectify that."

Rowyn paused beside a trash bin, pitched in her half-finished cone and accepted Darius's napkin to toss as well. Inside, the words she'd never verbalized churned in her chest like a furious cyclone, gathering momentum, ready to burst free. But fear corked the flood. She wanted to talk to Darius—confide in him—but an invisible hand covered her mouth, trapping the words.

With a light tug, he guided her back to the middle of the path. They resumed walking, her hand still firmly clasped in his.

"You know, I grew up in a family not so different from yours. We were prominent, well-to-do, in the clothing business. My father is third-generation Italian. His grandfather had emigrated from Italy and founded a department store that started with a wheeled cart full of shoes."

"He sounds like a remarkable, determined man."

"From the stories, that description's pretty accurate. He died when I was a baby. But my grandfather was just like him. Proud. Hard-working. Not free with praise, but when he gave it, it felt like the sky had just opened up and beamed down a gift." Darius chuckled. "I loved him, and though he never uttered the words, I know he loved me. Unfortunately my father could not say the same."

Caught up in his story, Rowyn hadn't noticed he'd paused beside one of the benches that dotted the trail. Darius lowered to the seat and gently pulled her down beside him. The wood warmed the underside of her thighs through the thin material of her dress and she leaned a shoulder against the back of the bench, her body turned toward him.

She hung on every word, hungry to learn more about this man who had captivated her from the first moment she'd noticed him standing at the end of the nightclub's bar.

"My father disappointed my grandfather. From his choice of wife, to anglicizing his name to 'Fury', to how he ran the family business. So he transferred his attention and time to me...and my father resented me for the approval he believed should've been his."

Darius flipped over the hand he held and, staring down at it, traced the light brown lines crisscrossing her pale palm. The tender touch tingled, transmitting hot pricks of pleasure to her breasts and between her thighs. She squirmed under the caress that, compared to others they'd shared, was almost platonic. But anything Darius did— from hand-holding to an innocent stroke across her palm— amounted to foreplay.

"Since I was old enough to understand, my father has been in competition with me. A spontaneous game of basketball turned into a vicious battle. When I brought home a report card full of A's and B's, he pulled out a report card from his childhood that contained straight A's. After I graduated from college and joined the company, he fought every promotion and bonus because he wanted me to earn my way through hard work and not nepotism, regardless if I remained in the office long after everyone had left or contributed to the rise in revenue for the entire year. His bitterness toward my grandfather never allowed us to have a relationship."

God, she understood that. Never being good enough. Never being able to attain approval, no matter the awards, accolades or success. Never receiving love from the one who was supposed to give it unconditionally.

She clenched her fingers into a fist, battling the urge to reach out and brush a caress down his cheek. Or stroke her thumb over one of those damn eyebrows. But years of rejection seemed like a manacle around her wrist, chaining her arm to her side.

Touch him. Comfort him. Give him what you've yearned for.

With a force of will that set her heart pounding in a frantic beat, Rowyn lifted her arm, extended her hand toward him and cupped his jaw. Displays of affection were as foreign to her as the Bible to an atheist. Sex with Darius had been a risk. She had shared and submitted her body to him in a way she'd never done with another man. Yet this small gesture left her more exposed and vulnerable than the hours she'd spent naked in his bed. It bared her heart, staked it to her chest—an easy target for rejection.

When Darius covered her hand with his then turned his head to place a kiss in the center of her palm, she sighed. And the band around her chest loosened.

"My mother resents me," she said softly. "Every time she looks at me, she's reminded of my father who she believes chose his family over her." The confession stumbled past her lips. For the first time, she admitted aloud the truth she'd known for more than half her life. Wanda understood the Harrisons weren't the happy-go-lucky unit they represented in pictures, but even she didn't know the extent of the antipathy.

Darius pressed his lips to her skin once more before lowering her hand to his thighs and cradling both. He waited, silent, his steady gaze centered on her face. In the blue depths of his eyes she didn't detect judgment or ridicule. Just compassion. Tenderness. And acceptance.

Those attributes gave her the strength to continue.

"My parents were young when they secretly married against his family's wishes. I'm sure Dad assumed they would accept her—and eventually me. But that never happened. They blamed Mom for leading their son astray, for trapping him, for not being Korean..." Rowyn choked out a humorless chuckle. "That he continued to work for the family business further complicated the situation and deepened the bitterness and anger that ultimately led to Mom leaving him."

"Your mother told you this?"

Rowyn shook her head. "No. Dad did a couple of years before he died." From her mother, Rowyn had heard curses, insults and rants about her selfish, worthless father who hadn't wanted either of them. Even to this day, eight years after his death, Pamela couldn't discuss her first husband rationally. "My parents divorced when I was eight and Mom did her best to keep me from him—changing the visitation dates, scheduling events on his weekends. A couple of times she forced me to call him and tell him I didn't want to see him. She needed to hurt him, and replacing him in his daughter's life with another father accomplished her goal."

In an abrupt motion, Rowyn lunged to her feet, unable to sit still any longer. It seemed as if a live wire vibrated under her skin. She needed to move, to do...something.

"Would you mind if we kept walking?"

"Not at all," Darius murmured. But instead of stepping out onto the path, he shifted in front of Rowyn, cupped her face between his palms and lowered his head until his forehead rested against hers. Slowly—so damn slowly—he brushed his lips over her mouth. Once. Twice. Then he dove deep, his tongue parting her lips and exploring what lay beyond.

He lit a match to the stick of her emotional dynamite and her control detonated into pieces around her feet. All the tension of the past minutes cracked under his caressing mouth and she arched into him, perched on her toes. She met him stroke for stroke. Sucked his tongue back into her mouth when he would've withdrawn. The hungry growl that rumbled in her throat should have embarrassed her. *Should* have. But it didn't. She needed him. Ached for him.

Craved the port he represented in the middle of her mental storm.

Darius lifted his head, ignoring her whimper of protest. And when she would have followed him, demanded he return to her, he pressed a thumb over her lips, denying her what she wanted most. The small, soft kiss he pressed to the corner of her mouth softened the blow of refusal.

"Finish it," he whispered and the quiet command was like a lance to a wound. The pain, anger and grief swelled and rushed out in a torrential outpour.

"I hurt him so badly. I hurt him," she blurted, speaking so fast the words tumbled over one another. She lifted her hands between them and placed them on his chest. She pushed, needing air, space...but he dropped his arms from her face and wrapped them around her to hold her tight. "I just wanted her to love me, to be nice to me. I couldn't make Daniel like me. All I had was her and she blamed me because Daniel wouldn't give me his last name or pay me the attention he lavished on Cindy. The only way I could make her happy was to reject Dad. She seemed to care then, to show me kindness. And I hurt one of the few people who loved me unconditionally." She wept, fisting the front of his shirt. "I never told him how sorry I was. He died not knowing I didn't mean those things I'd said. He never knew..."

Harsh sobs racked her body and she couldn't halt the tremors that attacked her. One moment she stood in Darius's arms and the next her feet left the ground and she was cradled to a hard chest. Soothing murmurs she couldn't decipher barely penetrated the grief that swept her away.

How much time passed, Rowyn couldn't say. But when the jagged weeping quieted into shallow, rough breaths that scratched her burning throat, she was once again on the bench they'd vacated. A solid shoulder supported her head and strong arms cuddled her close.

She remained in Darius' embrace, content, as if a huge boulder she'd carried for years had suddenly been hoisted from her chest. She felt...free.

And probably looked like a hot mess with swollen eyes, a puffy face and slinging snot. As if hearing her internal list, Darius handed her a white handkerchief. Rowyn murmured a "thank-you" then tried to clean up all vestiges of her breakdown.

He didn't speak, allowing her to gather her composure and thoughts, and she was grateful. God, she hadn't realized all that guilt, grief and anger had been caged in her like prisoners of war. Memories of her father and their short time together rose and for the first time she didn't suppress them. Their initial stilted lunch at one of the riverside cafés. She'd been nervous and so had he. But after an hour the walls had lowered and they had tentatively reached out to each other, planning another lunch date.

The images passed in a blurred succession. Lunch, dinner, shopping. Her twenty- second birthday. She touched her fingertips to the base of her throat. He'd given her the beautiful necklace with his native Korean engraved on the back. *To my princess.* Because she would never stop being his princess, he'd told her. He'd died three months later of a freak brain aneurysm.

Another sob, less intense than its predecessors, surged in her chest. Damn, she missed that necklace. Her last link to her father, gone. Unless…Shit, she was an idiot! Why hadn't she thought of it before?

She jerked her head up and met Darius' concerned, soft gaze. "Did you find a necklace at your place after I…uh…left?"

He arched his eyebrow and, for once, she didn't experience the urge to rip it off.

Now it seemed kind of adorable. "What?" he asked.

Rowyn gripped his shoulder. "Did you find a necklace?"

"A gold chain with a pendant?" He nodded. "Yes. You left it on my bedroom dresser."

Joy swelled and spilled over into a delighted cry. She threw her arms around him and squeezed him tight. With a startled bark of laughter, he clutched her to him. *Oh God,* she prayed. *Thank you, thank you.*

Grinning, she leaned back far enough to plant a huge, hard kiss on his smiling mouth.

"I take it you're happy," he drawled.

Rowyn mimicked the gesture she'd come to think of as his trademark and lifted her eyebrow. "What gave you that idea?"

He chuckled and swept a caress down her spine. "I don't know. The wild ecstatic shriek, the half nelson on my neck, the kiss…"

"I don't shriek," she informed him, but ruined the dignified denial with another hug. Happiness. It filled her to capacity, invading her lungs, replacing her breath. "The necklace. Can you mail it to me?"

"I can do better than that." He hitched his hip up and removed a slender cell phone from the front pocket of his pants. With one hand he tapped in a number and pressed the small phone to his ear. "Hey,

Valerie," he greeted. "I need a favor." Minutes later he ended his call, having instructed his assistant to pick up the jewelry from his house and overnight it that day.

"Thank you," Rowyn said, voice hoarse. So many words—*thank you for caring, thank you for holding me while I cried, thank you for finding that piece of my heart and protecting it*— jumbled in her head. And none of them could adequately express what he'd done for her. So she bowed her head, pressed her face to the warm crook of his neck and whispered it again. "Thank you."

Once more, he tucked her into the haven of his body, his arms a harbor that shouldn't have offered safety, shouldn't have provided protection.

It would be the height of stupidity to get used to Darius' arms around her.

She'd never considered herself a foolish woman… Guess it really was a day for "firsts."

CHAPTER FIVE

"However, this evening she lost track of time and left only at the final stroke of midnight..."—Cinderella

"I feel like Pretty Woman...but without the whole prostitute thing."—Rowyn Jeong

"Just give me about ten minutes to change clothes. Then we'll swing by your house so you can change, and then we can head out to dinner." Darius glanced over his shoulder as he swiped the magnetized key card through the electronic door slot. Reassured by Rowyn's nod, he pressed the handle down and pushed the hotel room door open.

They moved into the large and elegantly appointed living room. Boston's skyline at sunset presented a vibrant, gorgeous backdrop through the floor-to-ceiling windows. Darius crossed to one of the tables flanking the couch and tugged the chain on the lamp to illuminate the shadowed interior. He turned to her and his breath caught in his throat. Rowyn had that effect on him—she had since the moment he'd laid eyes on her months ago, sitting alone down the length of the nightclub bar.

Thinking back on how they'd met and spent their first—and only—night together, Darius could imagine why Rowyn believed he picked up women and often indulged in one-night stands. He wasn't a saint—his halo would've been repossessed a long time ago—but it had been years since he'd done anything so promiscuous. Rowyn had been the exception to the rule. And their time together would have exceeded more than a few hours if she had remained in his bed...remained with him.

No, he hadn't fallen in love with her that night. He studied the straight line of her spine as she crossed the room to stand before the window. But images of her, of those sex-filled hours, lingered in his head, never fading. And when he'd seen her the evening before in her parents' home, an inexplicable joy—as though he'd found something precious that had been lost to him—had seized hold of his chest.

Lost. It described the heartbroken woman he'd held in his arms on the park bench. Jesus. Those ragged cries had ripped his heart from his chest. Without conscious thought, he rubbed his breastbone and imagined he could massage away the echo of pain still resonating hours later. He would have given anything to shoulder her hurt and grief. Witnessing the proud, strong woman he'd come to know curl against him as if attempting to escape herself had stirred something in him—something that had lain dormant until that moment. Suddenly he yearned to protect, shelter...keep. He couldn't turn back time and wipe out her pain. But he could make damn sure it didn't touch her in the present or future.

Being able to offer her the necklace had transformed him into Hercules. He'd wanted to beg Rowyn to give him something else he could do for her. Just to see happiness light up her dark eyes again.

Damn, she was lovely. He stared at her striking profile. All sleek lines and gorgeous curves. The modest hem of her dress bared long, toned legs. He'd had the pleasure of those slender brown limbs locked around his waist, over his shoulders. He wanted that again. *Needed* it again. His cock hardened in complete agreement.

Lust tempered by a softer but no less intense emotion hummed through his body like an electrical current. Plans for dinner relegated to *later*, he approached her. In a replay of the night before, he paused behind her, close enough for the dark strands of her ponytail to tickle his chin. And he drew closer still, until her lower back cradled his straining dick and his chest pressed to her shoulder blades. Unlike last night, he didn't allow a polite distance between them. Nothing but her dress and his pants separated his cock from riding the shallow dip below her spine. It still wasn't enough. He rubbed his cheek against the heavy silk of her hair. It wouldn't be until her pussy surrounded his cock with its blistering heat.

"Are you smelling my hair again?"

He smiled at the softly spoken question, acknowledging the attempt at humor but detecting the shiver beneath. Trepidation or arousal? He clasped her waist, his thumbs meeting on the ridges of her spine. Yet he didn't linger. His breathing deepened as desire punched a hole in his stomach and he slid his hands up the sides of her slender torso, not stopping until he cupped the undersides of her generous breasts. Generous, *beautiful* breasts—he gave the mounds a light squeeze.

Rowyn stiffened, gasped and released the sweetest whimper he'd ever heard. It echoed the need that stiffened his cock, gripped his balls and twisted his gut.

"God, that's sweet," he murmured and flicked his thumbs across the hard nipples poking against the thin fabric of her dress. His reward came in the form of another needy moan. She dropped her head back and rested it on his shoulder. Quick bursts of air parted her lips and thick, black fans of lowered lashes hid her eyes. He pressed a kiss to her temple and, without words, declared how beautiful he found her. With his hands he worshipped her, molding her flesh, circling and then pinching the hard tips cresting her breasts.

The pained cries in no way resembled the sobs from that afternoon. Rowyn arched and twisted under his touch, then encircled his wrists like cuffs with her fingers. But not to restrain him. To hold on.

He nipped the curve of her ear. "Do you know how good you feel to me?" he rasped. "I could come just from squeezing these lovely breasts. Or your nipples." Darius released a rough, broken chuckle that sounded tormented to his ears. "I've dreamed about sucking your nipples, sweetheart. How they felt on my tongue. Sometimes I wake up savoring the imprint of them," he growled and rolled the stiff peaks, tugged them until she shuddered against him. The restless shifting of her thighs, the sensual roll of her hips—they all telegraphed her heightened lust. *So fucking responsive.* He gritted his teeth as her ass stroked his dick.

"Fuck this," he snapped and abandoned her breasts. Ignoring her whispered protest, he shifted backward and attacked his belt. In seconds he had the slim leather freed of its buckle, the pants closure open and zipper lowered. With one hand he reached inside his boxers and fisted his aching cock while with the other he shoved his pants and underwear beneath his balls.

"Lift your skirt." The guttural command reflected the hunger that flayed him. He wanted to give her tenderness—should have been controlled enough to do so—but it eluded him at the promise of being balls-deep inside her pussy after six long months of dreaming about it.

Rowyn obeyed. She clutched the skirt of her dress and bunched the material until the hem brushed the bottom curve of her ass. Then, like a seductive striptease, she revealed the perfect globes bared by a pink lace thong. Son. Of. A. Bitch.

A bead of precum appeared on his cock head.

"Now the panties, sweetheart," he encouraged, rocking his hips forward and thrusting his dick through his fist—a poor substitute for the wet, swollen flesh Rowyn slowly bared as she inched the lace underwear past her ass. "Don't let the dress go," he ordered when the skirt started to drift down. "Hold it up and bend over. I want to see your pussy."

Rowyn hesitated, the minute clenching of her fists around the dress hem a sign of uncertainly or embarrassment. Didn't she realize how hard she made him—how hot she made him burn? Shame on *him* if she doubted his desire or need for her.

"Do it, sweetheart." He rubbed his palm up the outside of her smooth thigh. The muscle tensed then relaxed. He continued the sensual exploration to her bare hip. "I've dreamed about your pretty pussy for months. I need to see, baby."

She gathered the skirt in front of her and bent over at the waist. Immediately he centered his gaze on the pink, swollen folds that glistened with her cream. He tightened his grip on his cock as Rowyn smoothed her thong down her slim thighs and exposed more of her lovely sex.

He couldn't help himself. Darius reached out and traced her slit with his forefinger. His balls drew up at the first touch of her flesh after so long. He groaned. Warm. Soft.

Heavy juices coated his fingertip and he stroked forward, covering the whole length of his finger in her wetness.

Rowyn flinched, a low, needy moan escaping her. She froze, clutching her ankles where her lacy panties pooled. Except for that small, initial jerk, she remained steady for his caress, her breath harsh pants in the otherwise silent room.

He strummed her clit once, twice. She repeated the low groan—the one that twisted his gut—but stayed motionless for his touch. As a reward, he gave the engorged nub a firmer touch. Her thighs quivered. He drew back, dragging moisture with him. And when he came to the tiny entrance of her pussy, he paused. Her breathing stilled. Darius tore his rapt attention away from her ass and the puffy lips and skimmed down.

The long tail of her hair fell over her shoulder and the tip brushed the floor. Her face was hidden from him as she pressed her forehead to her knees, but the slight arch of her back, the suspension of breath broadcasted her anticipation, her eagerness to be penetrated, filled.

He circled the opening and it clenched his fingertip. God, it was so small. His dick jerked under his palm as he thought of pressing into that hole, stretching it, being surrounded by it.

"Darius." Rowyn's muffled plea urged him to give her a deeper caress. But he resisted. "No," she protested as he abandoned her flesh, lifted his juice-covered finger to his mouth and slid it over his tongue.

Ignoring her whimper, he sucked her delicious cream clean and couldn't contain a hungry growl as her essence detonated on his tongue and filled his mouth. He wanted to dive back into her pussy for more. With regret, he pulled his finger free of his mouth.

"You taste so good," he murmured and lowered his hands to her waist. "Stand up, sweetheart." Rowyn straightened and stepped free of her underwear. The desire to finally see her naked again roared up in him and he submitted to the craving. He slid his thumbs under the straps of her dress, stroked them over her shoulders and down her arms. The thin material caught at her hips for a moment before joining the lace at her feet.

Leaning forward, he encircled her wrists and guided her arms above her head, flattening her palms to the window.

She was...*breathtaking*. With the setting sun illuminating her tall, elegant, curvaceous body, she resembled a pagan goddess ready—demanding—to be worshipped. He succumbed.

Darius pressed his lips to her nape. He followed the elegant length of her back to the dip at the base and then retraced the damp line, not pausing until he reached her neck once more.

"So lovely." With a reverent sigh, he cupped her breasts again, the nipples captured between his fingers. As he pinched the hard tips, he nestled his cock between her ass cheeks. Rowyn moaned and ground her hips back against his groin, pushing her breasts into his hands. He bent his knees and then slowly straightened, his shaft separating the shadowed cleft between her ass cheeks. The paler flesh of his dick parting the mocha skin of the rounded, firm globes struck him as beautiful. The perfect blending of rich color.

He held her tightly to him, gripping her soft flesh like an anchor as he pulled back, slid his shaft between her drenched pussy lips and coated his cock in her cream. Rowyn widened her stance as if in invitation to repeat the caress, but he again rode the dark slit of her ass. With a tortured groan, he released her breasts, palmed her cheeks and pressed them close together to form a tight channel for his aching dick.

"Fuck," he whispered as his cock head appeared and disappeared. Blood thundered in his head then rushed straight to his erection, filling it, hardening it more. His breath burst from his lips in harsh pants as electricity tingled at the small of his back and zinged to his balls. The slick warmth of her flesh surrounding his cock along with the visual stimulation dragged him to the edge of orgasm before casting him over with a hoarse roar.

His heart stopped, his hips jerked and his thigh muscles twitched with the force of release. Rowyn bucked beneath him, rocking her ass over his rigid length and wringing every drop of cum from his cock.

"Sweetheart." The endearment was all he could manage after the ecstasy he'd experienced. He leaned forward and rested his forehead on her shoulder. Aftershocks raced through his body, shivered over his skin. And still his hips worked at her ass in a lazy rhythm.

Several moments passed. Quiet claimed the room and, with a sigh, he straightened and shifted away. He gazed at her back and the milky evidence of his lust he'd shot all over her skin. He murmured an apology, yanked his shirt over his head and wiped away his semen. After hitching his pants and underwear up to his hips, he knelt and gathered her clothes from the floor and folded them over his arm. Then he rose to his feet, clasped one of her hands, lowered it from the window and turned her away from the glass to face him.

"Thank you," he said before taking her lips. He dipped his tongue into her mouth and tasted her sweetness. Rowyn arched up to meet his kiss and deepen it with a hunger that stirred the fire his release hadn't extinguished. She slanted her head and sucked on his tongue. And damn if the suckling motion didn't throb in his balls. "Come with me," he growled into her mouth.

Darius guided her across the room, and as they passed the couch, he tossed their discarded clothing on the armrest before continuing toward the bedroom.

They crossed the threshold and he closed the door behind them. In seconds, he dropped his pants and underwear to the floor and stood as naked as she. Her soft gasp seemed to resonate in the silent room like a shout across an empty stadium. She raised her eyes to meet his and he almost grabbed her to him. Need. Desire. Both darkened her gaze. Then she lowered her lashes and hid what his mind wanted to believe had also been tenderness.

Rowyn moved close, circled a fingertip around his nipple then raked a nail over the puckered tip. He sucked in a lungful of air and his gut clenched. The dusky peaks may have been smaller than her nipples, but they were no less sensitive. He wanted her mouth on him.

As if hearing his wish, she dipped her head to his chest and lapped at his flesh. He hissed in pleasure and clasped her head to him. She coiled her tongue around the hard bump, flicking and sucking.

"Here," he ordered and didn't wait way for her to obey but steered her head to the neglected tip. As she closed her teeth around it, he couldn't contain his rumble of pleasure. The woman's mouth should have been labeled a lethal weapon—lethal to his control, lethal to his sanity. Lethal to his soul.

He tugged her head up and crushed a kiss to her mouth. At the same time, he walked her backward until she bumped the edge of the mattress. As soon as she fell on the bed, he covered her—his mouth continued to maraud hers, his chest pressing her breasts, his thighs bracketing her legs, his cock grinding into the soft give of her stomach.

Rowyn tipped her chin up, disconnecting their mouths. She dragged in much- needed air. "Darius," she pleaded, clutching his firm ass, biting into the taut flesh with her fingernails and silently begging for the deeper, harder stroke of his cock in her pussy. She felt so empty. She needed to be penetrated, opened, stretched…filled. Her hips writhed underneath his and she tried to shift upward and maneuver his rigid length over her sex.

"No," he objected, nipping her jaw. "Not yet. I want to eat your sweet pussy before I fuck it." The blunt, sexual words almost hurtled her into orgasm. Her pussy spasmed and clenched. "Tell me you want it, sweetheart. Tell me you want my tongue deep inside you."

"Yes..." she moaned the reply and, as Darius slid down her body, planting kisses between her breasts and on her stomach, she scratched his back and shoulders. "Please, Dar—"

The first swipe of his tongue through her slit tore a piercing scream from her throat. Her back arched off the mattress and he grasped her hips to hold her still for his mouth. His hungry rumble vibrated in her sex.

"God, it's good." He stabbed at her clit with his tongue then curled it around the sensitive nub. She jolted beneath him and he tightened his grip. Ruthlessly he lashed and suckled, driving her to the very brink before drawing her back, only to start all over again. Yet when he tilted her hips at a higher angle and slanted his head to thrust his tongue into the entrance to her pussy, she came undone.

Pleasure consumed her, coursed through her like a living thing. It seemed as if she became a being without thought, one who existed solely on feeling and emotion. She writhed and bucked, hoarse cries falling from her lips and punctuating the wet sounds of his suction on her pussy. Against her protests, he withdrew from her sheath. After murmuring a low reassurance, he latched on to her clit once more and buried two fingers in her pussy. Rowyn released a strangled cry and rocked her hips in time to the hard thrusts.

"Darius," she begged, clawing at the bed sheets. "Please let me come. I need to..." The tempo increased—he flicked faster and finger fucked her harder. The orgasm swirled low in her back, her pelvis. Like a runaway train picking up speed, it rocketed closer and closer until...

She screamed. Her body stiffened, jerked. Release rolled through her, over her. Darius nursed it, lapping at her clit, stimulating her sex with slow, shallow stabs of his fingers, bringing her down but also building the pleasure up again.

"I need to be inside you," he growled and jackknifed off the bed. In seconds he'd grabbed his pants off the floor then removed his wallet and the condom tucked in the fold. With hurried movements, he sheathed his cock with the latex and climbed back onto the mattress. He knelt between her spread legs and rubbed his hands up her calves to her inner thighs. He brushed the crease where her legs and torso met with his fingertips. "Wider, sweetheart. Open up for me."

Heart pounding, she stared up at him and submitted to his command. Anticipation—and just a bit of feminine apprehension—fluttered in her stomach. But the hunger to have his cock spread her with its special burn, taking her to the delicious edge that rode pain and pleasure, overrode everything else. She needed it—longed for it.

"Please," she whispered and held her arms outstretched to him, inviting him into her embrace. Her personal space. She wanted to breathe him in, the scent of sand and sex that clung to his skin. Darius accepted the invitation, sliding over her and melding his mouth to hers in a kiss that spoke of lust and passion. Yet the tender glide of his lips—once, twice, before his tongue plunged deep—hinted at a gentleness that exceeded need.

He pressed his chest to her breasts and she couldn't help but subtly twist her torso to rub her hard, aching nipples over his muscles. She gasped as the spear of pleasure shot directly from the stiff tips to her pulsing clit. With a tilt of her pelvis, she stroked her drenched folds over his cock. The pressure dragged a long moan from her.

Darius continued to make love to her mouth as he planted his hands on either side of her head and levered his torso off hers. A moment later, his cock head prodded her pussy. *Finally.* She tore her mouth away from his and turned her head to the side, eyes squeezed shut.

"Uh-uh." The low, sexy tone licked over her skin seconds before his tongue blazed a path up her neck to nip her earlobe. "Don't turn away. It's you and me."

"I'm not turning away," she contradicted his assumption. Rowyn returned her gaze to his and drank in the gleaming blue eyes, kiss-swollen lips, flushed cheekbones and hard jaw. "I just want to remember every moment. For later."

He stared down at her, silent for several long seconds. Then he lowered his lashes, bent his head, brushed a soft caress over her brow—and thrust forward.

She gasped. Her neck arched and she clutched his arms in a hang-on-for-dear-life grip. So full. God, so good.

"I want in, Rowyn," he demanded softly in her ear. "Six months, sweetheart. I want in now." He nipped the curve of her ear and laid a kiss just below her lobe, steadily surging forward and withdrawing. With each thrust and retreat, he claimed more of her pussy. The heavy weight of his cock and the power of each stroke stretched her sex and she spasmed around his hard stalk. He gave her less time to become accustomed to the invasion but Rowyn found she didn't need it. No, she'd longed for the steady pleasure- pain burn, welcomed it.

"That's it." The praise delivered in the tender but rough voice thrilled her, arrowing a shaft of delight from her heart to the hot, wet place he fucked with determination. "Damn, you're tight. And so wet. A little more, sweetheart. Just a little..."

He flexed his hips and groaned. His body stiffened over her. The mask of passion that claimed his face captured her fascination. Lips drawn into a tight line, teeth clenched so hard a tiny muscle jumped along the strong line of his jaw. Nostrils flared and dark lashes lowered in a hooded, sensual stare that had her pussy clenching around his fully embedded cock. A long, low hiss escaped his lips and blue fire leaped in his eyes.

She lifted her legs and locked her ankles just above his tight ass. A raw, hungry growl rumbled in his chest and as he shifted, his heavy sac grazed the stretched folds of her sex. Another sensation to add to the ecstasy overload she found herself tossed into. She stared into the face of desire, her pussy filled to capacity with it. She took in a deep breath and inhaled the scent of sex from his skin—and still she craved more.

"Are you okay?" he asked. She registered the question, but how the hell did he expect her to answer when he did that circle thing with his hips, setting her clit on a one-way ticket to orgasm? She couldn't reply, so instead she squeezed the muscles in her sex, clamping down on his cock. When he grunted above her, Rowyn figured he received his answer.

"Fuck," he muttered and proceeded to do just that—fuck her. He rode her hard. With every long, plunging stroke of his cock he shoved her closer to the precipice of release. She cried out, sobbing her pleasure that penetrated not only her flesh but her heart, her soul.

The mattress bounced beneath them. The headboard banged out the wild rhythm he set with his driving hips. And she held on to him through it all, trusting where he would take her. As the orgasm swelled, it seemed almost frightening in its intensity, in its power. Yet she threw herself headfirst into the blaze, knowing—believing—he would be there to catch her.

CHAPTER SIX

"The prince chased her, but outside the palace, the guards had seen only a simple country wench leave. The prince pocketed the slipper and vowed to find and marry the girl to whom it belonged."—Cinderella

"Not this shit again."—Darius Fiore

The aroma of freshly brewing coffee tickled his nose and Darius inhaled. Damn. Smelling it was like foreplay to the main event—that first delicious cup.

He reached over his head, opened the cupboard door and removed two mugs the hotel provided. As he waited for the pot to finish, he glanced toward the closed bedroom door. He regretted not leaving it open so he could look in on the sleeping figure of the woman who'd shared his bed and her body with him last night. Unlike the previous time they'd been together, he'd woken up next to her this morning. A grin curved his lips. Who would've guessed Rowyn Jeong was a cuddler?

The last of the coffee trickled into the pot, and after filling both ceramic cups with the dark brew, he added cream and sugar to one and left the other black. On bare feet, he turned and exited the small kitchenette, mugs in hand. He'd barely made it across the living area when a knock sounded on the hotel room door. Frowning, he shot a glance at the digital clock on the kitchenette counter. 7:56 a.m. Who could that be?

Darius set the steaming cups on the small table beside the couch and headed toward the door. With a twist of his wrist he had the lock unbolted and the door opened. Surprise sang through him.

Cindy Harrison.

Rowyn's younger sister smiled up at him, lovely and fresh in a yellow summer dress that complimented her caramel skin. Her dark hair curled around her shoulders and framed a face that most likely mesmerized every man she met.

Except him.

She didn't have hair that fell down her back in a waterfall of dark silk. Her eyes, while a very pretty hazel, didn't possess the striking tilt of the outer corners. Nor were they the beautiful, mysterious brown that could gleam with passion or blaze with anger. Cindy's petite slenderness couldn't compare to the statuesque, curvy body that seemed built for fucking...for loving.

No. Cindy, with her traditional loveliness, didn't hold a torch— fuck, a candle—to her older sister.

"Can I come in?" she asked, flashing the dimples in her cheeks.

"Of course." Darius shifted back and allowed enough room for her to enter the hotel suite. Her gaze dropped and flicked over his bare chest and the black pants he'd dragged on but had left unbuttoned. Hell, he'd intended to wear them only long enough to make coffee. Spending the morning making love to Rowyn didn't require clothes.

"I woke you," she apologized, stepping past him. "I wanted to catch you before you started your day."

"No, it's fine," Darius said. *As long as we get this over with quickly.* "What can I do for you?"

Cindy wheeled around on her dainty heels, her smile widening. "I'd like to invite you to breakfast and then show you our beautiful city."

The irony over how her ploy mirrored the one he'd sprung on Rowyn the day before amused him. At least he'd brought coffee, while Cindy had shown up empty- handed.

"That's very considerate of you, but actually, I toured Boston yesterday." He slid his hands into the front pockets of his pants. "And you're right. Your city is beautiful."

"Oh." She pouted and he had a hard time determining if her disappointment was genuine. "Well the offer for breakfast is still open. I would love to treat you to a hot meal and spend time getting to know you before you leave." She moved closer to him, lowering her lids as she raised a hand and laid her fingers on his chest. "We won't have an opportunity to be alone at Daddy's party tonight." She lifted her lashes and traced a small pattern over his skin. "I really would like that...quality time with you."

Well shit. Wasn't this just...awkward.

"Cindy," he said and moved backward. Her arm fell to her side and a faintly puzzled frown creased her brow as if she couldn't comprehend his lack of response to her touch. "I appreciate the offer. I do. But I have to decline. Thank you, though."

"I don't underst—" She narrowed her gaze on the table beside him. The table where he'd placed the two coffee mugs before answering the door. A moment of silence passed as her scrutiny skipped over the couch and—dammit—landed on the discarded clothes draped across the sofa arm.

Fuck.

Her hazel eyes returned to him. He braced himself for indignation and was taken aback by the delight that twinkled in her eyes. She smiled and an inexplicable sense of foreboding fluttered in his stomach.

"It seems I do understand after all," she murmured. "Rain check on the breakfast? Maybe the next time you're in town?"

Darius nodded, still confused by her reaction, but the man in him who cringed at the thought of female hysterics was grateful. "Count on it."

"I'll see you tonight, then." She turned and, with a wiggle of her fingers, waved good-bye and left the suite.

Darius remained rooted next to the couch. He stared at the spot where Cindy had stood, bemused. And he'd considered Rowyn an enigma. Apparently her stepsister shared the trait. With a shrug, he picked up the still-warm cups and headed toward the bedroom. And the woman sleeping there. And thoughts of waking her up with coffee. Followed by hours of sex, sweat and tangled sheets.

With the skill a juggler would have envied, he balanced the two mugs in one hand and twisted the doorknob with the other. The second shock of the day resonated through him and panic nipped at its heels. He imagined how he appeared, standing in the doorway, holding coffee and staring at Rowyn as she roamed about the room in the robe the hotel provided. Preparing to run. Again.

Hurt and anger grappled for dominance until he couldn't distinguish one from the other. They melded into a fiery mass that lodged under his breastbone.

After what they'd shared yesterday and last night, she would still run from him. Still jump from their bed and leave him as if he were that one-night stand when she had become so much more to him.

"Going somewhere?" he asked, brow arched as he set the cups on the long dresser nearest the door. His mild tone didn't betray the emotion that blistered his chest.

"That was Cindy," she said and crossed her arms in a gesture that seemed less defiant and more protective. "I have to get out of here."

"Your sister is gone." He dropped his hands to the pants zipper and, in a deliberate motion, lowered it. The only sound that penetrated the stillness in the room was the rasp of the metal teeth separating. Rowyn's gaze followed the motion and widened in alarm.

"What are you doing?" she asked sharply.

Darius didn't answer, letting his actions speak for themselves as he lowered the pants down his hips and thighs. He stepped free of the material and stood before her bare-ass naked. Her stare jerked from his hardening dick back to his face. Her expression of dismay and arousal would have been amusing if he wasn't so damn pissed.

On silent feet, he stalked across the small space between them. He assumed her surprise allowed him to tug the terrycloth belt free, but her paralysis lasted only a moment. Rowyn clutched the lapels to her throat with both hands.

"Darius," she protested as he gripped the material under her fists and pried the robe loose. "We can't..." The words died on her lips as the cloth slipped down her arms and pooled on the floor behind her.

"Yes?" He stepped forward. And groaned. Her breasts with their hard dark nipples pressed to his chest chased away his hurt and anger. A gnawing hunger remained. A hunger he'd believed had been satisfied countless times the night before. He was beginning to think it could never be sated. He'd be granted a respite maybe, but never fully gratified.

He ground his cock against the softness of her stomach. On a low growl, he cupped her ass and held her still as he circled his hips, stroking his dick against her, needing the sweet pleasure of skin-to-skin contact. With a soft, ravenous moan, Rowyn surrendered. She lifted her arms and wound them around his neck. Their mouths met halfway. Tongues dueled, entwined and licked. He changed the angle of his head and dove deeper, demanding all she had to give him. Her taste. Her moans. Her submission...her heart.

In moments, Darius lowered Rowyn to the bed. She spread her thighs wide and he settled into the natural vee and welcoming heat of her pussy. The swollen lips gloved his cock and he couldn't resist sliding his shaft through the wet slit. He grunted with pleasure. She whimpered as his cock head bumped over her engorged clit. The pretty pink button he'd sucked and teased countless times hours before peeked from between the folds as if begging for attention. Shifting up, he ground the base of his cock against it and satisfaction surged through him at Rowyn's hoarse cry. With a low curse, he rolled off her and reached for one of the condoms he'd tossed on the bedside dresser at some point during the night. In seconds, he tore the small foil packet open, rolled the lubricated latex over his erection and returned to the woman on the bed who represented ecstasy and paradise. The breath hissed from between his lips as he reclaimed his position between her thighs.

"Listen to me," he demanded and cupped her face, holding her head captive between his palms. Her lashes fluttered then lifted and he stared down into her glazed eyes. "*Here* is where you belong." He emphasized "here" with a small movement of his hips, and then penetrated her pussy with one hard thrust that sheathed half his erection. "And *here* is where I belong." Again he punctuated the word with another stroke that buried him balls-deep inside her sex. Her shocked gasp heated his lips as, for the first time, she took his cock in two short thrusts.

"There you go," he whispered and dipped in her mouth for a short kiss. "Fuck, I can feel your pussy shivering around my dick, baby." He groaned and pressed his forehead to hers. "This is where *we* belong." He rolled his hips and stroked his pelvis over her clit. When she lifted her legs and encircled his waist, the balls of her feet settling in the small of his back for a long ride, he withdrew, emitting a groan at the exquisite pleasure of her flesh dragging over his sensitive shaft. "Don't try to leave again, Rowyn," he murmured, voice hoarse with lust and a fierce need that had nothing to do with his cock and everything to do with his heart. "I won't let you go again."

And with that promise thrown between them, he proceeded to make love to her, branding her as she'd already done to him.

* * * * *

"Thank you." Rowyn nodded as she accepted the glass of champagne from the server. God, she hated these tedious parties. She lifted the drink to her lips and sipped, not in the mood for the alcohol or the social event. She would have preferred to remain locked up Darius' hotel room with him. Or over him. Under him.

A small smile curved her lips. She hid it behind the rim of her glass, but nothing could suppress the warmth that unfurled in her belly. The last two days had been...magical. From walking among the shops of Boston hand-in-hand to the hours of hot sex...No. Not sex. Making love.

For her, she'd made love last night and this morning. In one afternoon, Darius knew her like no other person. His compassion and kindness had rubbed balm over the wounds in her soul and his touch had conveyed how special he found her. Rowyn had felt beautiful. Even...loved.

She slammed the mental brakes and skidded all over the road called "happily ever after." One night—okay, two and a half days—didn't make their ending a fairy tale.

Let's face it. I've known so little love, it would be a simple leap to confuse affection and great sex with something deeper. Don't be a fool.

Her smile dimmed. Pamela, her mother, couldn't give her love. What made her think Darius would?

"You look like you have the weight of the world on your shoulders," Wanda said in lieu of greeting as she pressed her cheek to Rowyn's. "Someone with champagne in her hand should not appear so serious."

Rowyn snorted. "I'm just answering the royal decree to attend this event. I have exactly"—she shot a discreet glance at her wrist—"one hour and forty-three minutes before I can leave."

"Come on, Ro," her friend drawled. "One would think you weren't excited to be here." They stared at each other for a long second before snickering into their champagne glasses.

"When did you get here?" Rowyn asked.

"About fifteen minutes ago." Wanda fell silent and—her brown-eyed gaze inscrutable—studied Rowyn. "I heard about the potential merger. And the women's fashion division being the guinea pig."

Rowyn shrugged with forced nonchalance. That particular knife had yet to be yanked from her heart. "It's Daniel's company to run as he sees best." The company line. And so much bullshit.

"That's bullshit," Wanda snapped, echoing her thought. Her friend edged closer and lowered her voice, but her fury rang as clear as a bell. "He is your stepfather. There were other departments to consider and choose from. Departments almost as profitable too. I bet he didn't even tell you what he'd planned." At Rowyn's silence, Wanda's full lips thinned into an angry slash. "What an inconsiderate, conniving asshole."

"Inconsiderate, yes. But not conniving," Rowyn contradicted and earned a glare for the effort.

"You're defending him?" The other woman's voice dropped to an ominous level and Rowyn smiled. To be championed was a rare occurrence and her friend's rage on her behalf felt...well...good.

"No." She shook her head. "I'm not defending him. But to call him conniving suggests he actually contemplated how I would feel and made a decision to be sneaky. Daniel didn't even *consider* me in his decision. I was a nonfactor."

"That's worse." Wanda inhaled, held it, and released the breath in a slow, deliberate exhalation. "No," she growled, "what's worse is your bitchy sister making the rounds, spreading rumors that you slept with the businessman your father is courting for the merger. According to her vicious gossip, you're trying to land this deal on your back."

"What?" The word exploded from Rowyn's lips on a hard gust of breath. Fingers of ice clawed at her, freezing the blood in her veins. "Darius?"

"Darius?" Wanda repeated. Confusion wrinkled her brow seconds before surprise swept it away. "Do you mean the Darius you met in Seattle last year?"

Rowyn nodded and uttered a faint, "Yes." She skimmed the room, the ice in her belly and chest reaching for her throat. For the first time, she noticed the sly glances or careful avoidance of eye contact.

No. Why would Cindy...? Rowyn closed her eyes. Her stepsister's voice drifted past her ears as if the younger woman stood right next to her.

It seems I do understand after all...

Oh   God.   Cindy—sweet,   butter-won't-melt-in-her-mouth, Cindy—had fucked her.

"Rowyn."

As her heart executed a swan dive toward her feet, she turned around to face her mother's pinched, thin-lipped face.

"In the study," she snapped, her black eyes glinting with fury. "Now."

* * * * *

By the time Rowyn closed the study door, she couldn't shake the illusion she'd just survived a gantlet of stares and whispers. Each pointed look and hushed comment slapped and punched at her, leaving invisible but very real bruises to her pride.

And it isn't over yet. She drew back her shoulders, fixed her I-don't-give-a-fuck mask firmly in place and faced the family that stood across the room as one unit—against her.

"Rowyn," Pamela began, "I have never been more ashamed of you than I am at this moment." Contempt dripped from her voice and it wounded Rowyn more than she cared to admit. Not the words or even the scorn—those she was used to. Her mother's quick acceptance of Rowyn's alleged crime, though...it most likely never occurred to Pamela to give her daughter the benefit of the doubt. Or even defend her character.

"Convicted without a trial, I see," she murmured.

Pamela slashed a hand through the air, cutting through Rowyn's protest. "Do you deny that you slept with Darius Fiore?" she asked, eyes narrowed. "And before you lie, consider that we would not confront you if we didn't have a reliable source about your actions."

Inside, Rowyn snorted. Like hell. The validity of the source or the information didn't matter one damn to them. It was the embarrassment of being whispered about that had tried, convicted and hanged Rowyn. And the source—she studied Cindy— wasn't that reliable.

Her stepsister wore the appropriate concerned-and-disappointed expression. Yet beneath the slightly troubled frown, her eyes gleamed with a satisfaction and malice Rowyn had always known existed beneath her sweet exterior. From the time Rowyn had entered Daniel and Cindy's home, the younger girl had perfected her innocent persona while all along playing cruel games.

Daniel, so besotted with the child by his beloved first wife, didn't perceive how Cindy monopolized his affection, gently demanding his attention so he wouldn't give too much to his new wife. He didn't catch on to her seemingly guileless comparisons of her mother and Pamela, until finally he found himself married to an embittered woman who hadn't been able to compete against her first husband's family, and now couldn't win the love of her current husband from his dead wife.

Cindy delighted in drama, unhappiness and confusion—especially if she was the maestro behind the discord.

Her stepsister met her stare and a tiny smile lifted a corner of the younger woman's mouth.

"Well?" Pamela demanded. "Do you deny it?"

"No," Rowyn answered, voice steady. "I don't."

"You slut," her mother spat. Rage contorted her features and, for the first time, Rowyn recognized the hatred that ate at the older woman like a cancer. Hatred for the daughter who was a constant reminder of her failure as a woman and a wife. Hatred for the life that should have been happy but instead had become a miserable prison where she abused alcohol to escape. Hatred for herself.

"I'm sorry, Daddy," Cindy said, regret heavy in the soft tone. "I didn't want to hurt you, but I thought you should know. I wish I hadn't recognized Rowyn's purse and keys. I wish…" Misery etched Cindy's features as if being the bearer of bad news tortured her.

Rowyn's palms itched to strangle the deceitful bitch.

"I wish you had come to me with your suspicions, Cindy," Rowyn said. "Then I could have explained my being with Darius had nothing to do with your father's company or the merger. He and I met months ago."

"Liar," her mother accused. "If that's true, why didn't you say something Thursday night?"

"Because it was, and is, our business," she countered coldly.

"You are just like your father," Pamela ranted. "Selfish. A liar. I should have left you with him, you ungrateful—"

"Be. Quiet."

Pamela gasped, eyes wide in shock over Rowyn's boldness. That made two of them. As often as she'd desired to, Rowyn had never interrupted or outright contradicted her mother. No matter how nasty the woman jabbed at her. But suddenly a lifetime of grief, resentment and hurt welled up inside and swept free caution like debris dragged away by the waters of a flood.

No more. She refused to be her mother's punching bag any longer. Yes. She was like her father. Loyal. Fair. Loving. And she deserved to be loved. Rowyn had given this family everything. And every one of them had either rejected her affection and hard work or had taken it selfishly as if *she* should be thankful they deigned to accept it.

No longer would she cast her heart before them. Rowyn had worth, value. And if they were too blind to see it then…

Then fuck them.

Daniel cleared his throat and the sound seemed to reverberate in the tomblike quiet.

"Even if what you say is true, Rowyn,"—though his tone suggested he didn't believe it any more than her mother did—"I'm afraid the damage has been done. Under the circumstances, I'm going to have to insist you step down from your position while the merger is in process. We cannot afford the hint of scandal. I hope you understand."

Yes, she did. All too well.

"Oh I do," Rowyn said. "I understand that I have lived as your stepdaughter for twenty years. I worked for you, headed the most productive department and led the company in profits for the past three years. And I didn't do it for the title or the money. I did it for you." A short bark of laughter burst from her throat at Daniel's confused frown. Because he had never offered her his affection, he didn't comprehend how she had willingly tried to give him hers. "I not only step down, Daniel, I quit. And not because I have anything to be ashamed of, because I don't."

Rowyn inhaled and met each pair of eyes that stared at her in varying degrees of astonishment and anger.

"I refuse to be part of a company that will accept rumor over fact without even giving a dependable, exemplary employee the courtesy of defending herself. And I refuse to be part of a family who takes for granted and despises the daughter and sister I've tried to be. In other words…" She hitched her chin up and, in spite of her pounding heart, declared, "I'm through with all of you."

"Don't be ridiculous," Pamela scoffed.

"I don't think she's being ridiculous at all," a soft voice

commented from behind Rowyn.

Startled, she whirled around. Darius stood just inside the open door. Formidable in a black jacket, shirt and pants, his brown curls brushed away from his striking face, his presence seemed to shrink the large study to the size of a closet.

He flicked his gaze to her face. Fury burned behind his impassive demeanor. There was nothing calm about the emotion that seethed in his blue eyes.

"Are you okay?" he murmured.

For a moment, an intense swell of I-am-so-falling-in-love-with-you struck her speechless. Her avenging dark angel.

He arched that damn—wonderful—eyebrow.

The smile that curved her lips originated in her heart, the eddy of warmth spreading to every part of her body. She was better than okay. So much better.

She nodded and, appearing satisfied, Darius returned his attention to her mother, Daniel and Cindy. Rowyn faced her family again. This time apprehension didn't clutch her heart as if she stood before a firing squad—not with Darius at her back.

"Darius." Daniel's joviality didn't conceal the strain that tightened his smile or the nervous leap of his Adam's apple as he swallowed convulsively. "We apologize for this." He loosed a false hearty laugh. "Just a little family issue, but I assure you it does not affect our professional relationship at all."

"But it does," Darius stated. Rowyn blinked. Was that a flinch? Did her stepfather actually just *flinch* under the lash of Darius' hard voice? "A businessman who cannot recognize the contribution of his employee or the caliber of her performance is shortsighted at best and grossly incompetent at worst. And I refuse to do business with him." The lapel of his jacket brushed her skin—bared by her backless dress—as he shifted closer. "But she is more than your employee or the head of the women's fashion department. Rowyn is your daughter. And that alone requires your loyalty. If you have none for your daughter, why should I believe you would have any for me?"

He didn't give Daniel an opportunity to reply. Heat from his touch penetrated her dress to the flesh beneath as he settled his hands on her hips.

"I pity you. All of you." As he pressed against her, the timbre of his voice vibrated from his chest through her back. Rowyn leaned into him, trusting him to support her physically as he did emotionally. "For years you had a daughter and sister ready and willing to love you, and each of you rejected her time and again."

"You have been in our home a handful of hours and have the audacity to judge us? You know nothing." Pamela sneered. Rage mottled her features and Rowyn realized she could count on one hand the number of times she'd witnessed a true smile on her mother's face. Not the social, bogus caricature, but a genuine smile full of joy and laughter.

God. She inhaled, breathed deep past the fist that seemed to squeeze her heart. What pain Pamela must have endured every day to exude such anger and misery. She drank to escape the ache of living as the "other woman" to a dead wife. The real tragedy was Rowyn had been there, trying to love and accept her all along.

"It's sad, isn't it?" Darius asked softly. "In the short amount of time I've known your daughter, I value her more than you do."

Without another word, he slipped his hand over hers and, with a small tug, turned her around. He grasped the doorknob, twisted it and opened the study door. The tinkle of laughter and hum of conversation poured into the room. They stepped through the entrance and Darius pulled the door closed behind them, leaving her family—and her past—behind.

"Come with me," he said and guided her through the crowd. They received curious and smug glances, but Rowyn didn't allow them to upset her. Not when Darius' hand was wrapped tightly around hers.

A couple of minutes later, she stood with him at the bottom of the steps outside her parents' home. A lovely, cool breeze wafted through the hot June night, caressing her bare shoulders like a lover's kiss. Like Darius' kiss.

She shivered and lifted her gaze to his. He stood in front of her, silent. "Thank you."

"I'm sorry."

His grin matched hers as their words jumbled over one another's. Darius inclined his head. "You first," he offered.

"Thank you," she repeated. "For coming to my defense. No one has done that for me before. And I want to…thank you."

He snorted. "I was apologizing for interfering in what may not have been my business." He lifted his hand and palmed her cheek, his fingertips stroking her temple. "You are very welcome."

Without giving thought to rejection or doubt, Rowyn turned her face into his palm and pressed her lips to the center. It still wasn't easy, this public-displays-of-affection thing. But Darius made trying worth the effort.

"I don't want to say good bye to you again." He lifted his other hand, and then her face was cradled between both palms, her head tilted back for the kiss he swept across her mouth. "I came here tonight with the intention of convincing you not to drop out of my life again. But after that," he jerked his chin in the direction of the house behind her, "I want more. Come to Seattle, Rowyn."

Her breath caught in her lungs then escaped on a rush of wind. The drumbeat of blood rushing through her veins resounded in her head. She lifted her hands to his arms and clasped the hard muscles. "Darius—"

"I'm not a fool like Daniel. I recognize a gifted businesswoman when I see one. I want to offer you the same position with my company you have with Harrisons'. I won't lie, Rowyn. The job is only a bribe to convince you to move. To be with me."

A quick flash of fear flared in her stomach. Fear of taking this huge, impulsive step.

Fear of leaving behind all she'd known. Fear of how much she hungered to say yes. "Don't think, sweetheart," he whispered. His blue eyes burned down into hers, entrapping her with their fire so she couldn't look away. "Don't use that beautiful, brilliant mind of yours. Speak from your heart. What does your heart say?"

Her heart. Her heart said..."Yes."

Joy lit his face and in that moment, all doubt and insecurities were carried away with the evening breeze. As his mouth covered hers and his tongue dipped inside to tangle, dance and discover, she was fine with not being able to map out and analyze the next step in her future. As long as it included this man, she was willing to take the chance.

And hey, she had a job waiting for her. She grinned under his kiss and Darius drew back to return her smile.

"I have something for you."

"Gifts already?" She perched on her toes and nipped the sensual curve of his bottom lip. "You've given me a job. What's next? The corner office?"

"No," he drawled with a shake of his head. "That belongs to me. I will let you seduce me in it, though."

Rowyn snickered and waited as he slipped his hand into his front pocket. "You are all," her eyes widened, "heart," she finished hoarsely, her gaze riveted on the delicate gold chain and pendant that dangled between his fingers.

Tears clogged her throat. Trembling, she touched a fingertip to the tiny crown etched into the jewelry's smooth surface. Memories flooded her, and suddenly she stood with her father eight years ago as he smiled and watched her open his gift.

I love you, Daddy. And I miss you.

Darius fastened the chain around her neck and the pendant felt familiar against her collarbone. Like a homecoming.

"It's a perfect fit," he murmured.

"Yes," Rowyn agreed and lifted her gaze to meet the quiet joy in his. "We are."

EPILOGUE

"No, open your eyes," he murmured. "I want to see."

Rowyn obeyed the low command and lifted her lashes even as her pussy pulsed with echoes of the orgasm that had just ripped through her body. The soft glow of the lamp on the desk cast its golden glow over Darius' face and chest as he leaned forward, and she remembered another time when he had issued the same demand. And he was just as beautiful now as he'd been that first night they'd spent together. His lips gleamed with her cream and the stark white of his gaping shirt was a sharp contrast against his golden skin. God, he was beautiful.

She uncurled her fingers from the edge of the desk above her head and flexed the stiff digits.

"See what?" she asked and lowered her arms. She fiddled with the top button of her silk shirt. He narrowed his gaze on the gesture. She smiled and pushed the first disc through the eyelet. In seconds, the shirt gapped wide.

"Go ahead," he ordered softly. Rowyn complied. As he lowered his hands to the thin leather belt at his waist, she opened the bra snap between her breasts and peeled the cups to the side. His soft growl

170

filled the room and renewed desire flooded her pussy as she fixed her gaze on his movements, waiting for the first glimpse of his cock. Darius released the buckle and dragged the zipper down, then reached inside his slacks and pulled his dick free.

She slicked her tongue over her lips, hungry. Again. The thick column of flesh capped with that smooth, bulbous head never failed to send a spear of lust straight to her pussy. He stroked his hand up the ridged length and her groan joined his. She palmed her breasts and pinched the nipples. *Oh God.* She rolled her hips and arched her back. It was so good. It was always this good with him.

"You know what I want to see?" he asked, his voice a husky caress over her sweat- dampened skin. Darius gripped the root of his cock and with a jerk of his hips, impaled her pussy. She pressed her head into the hard wood of the desk and a cry tore from her throat. "That," he grunted, drew back and thrust forward again. "That's what I need."

He loomed over her, his palms flattening next to her head and his arms caging her. In the warm lamplight, the wide gold band gleamed on the ring finger of his left hand. The sight of it pleasured her as much as the cock that parted her swollen pussy. She closed her eyes and this time Darius didn't demand she reopen them. He rested his forehead against hers and their breath mingled.

"Open for me, sweetheart," he whispered. Eager, she lifted her legs and locked her ankles behind his back. She clutched his arms and held on to him as if he were her port in an erotic storm. The base of his cock ground against her clit and shoved her closer to the orgasm that hovered just out of reach.

"Darius," she pleaded, straining toward him.

"I have you." He took her mouth in a burning, hard kiss. "I have you, sweetheart."

She gave herself over to him. He rode her hard, fast. He plunged his cock over and over into her pussy, stoking a fire that roared into a conflagration and consumed her in its flames. Her scream echoed in the shadowed office as Darius urged her to take more, go for more. He continued to fuck her and before her heart slowed after the first orgasm, another rocketed through her. This time Darius followed her. He threw his head back and his dick jerked and pulsed inside her sex, hot spurts of semen flooding her rippling flesh.

Rowyn held him as he bucked and shivered above her. When he

settled his weight over her, skimmed soft lips over her jaw and murmured words that were lost against her skin, she smiled.

"Do you think everyone knows what goes on in your office when we 'work late'?" she asked, rubbing her palm over his dark waves.

His smile tickled her skin as he swept his lips over her cheekbone.

"What a man and wife do together is their own business...even if it is in the office."

"Right." Rowyn chuckled and the pleasure that shivered through her had more to do with the man pressed to her than the words he'd whispered in her ear. Sometimes it was hard to believe Darius had reentered her life only eighteen months ago. So much had changed, the least of the adjustments being her relocation from Boston to Seattle. The biggest transformation had been her.

No longer under the dysfunctional influence of her family, she'd become the woman she'd dreamed of being for so long. Open. Carefree. Confident. Beautiful. Darius had not only offered her a top position in his company, he'd given her something more valuable. Laughter. Trust. Faith. Joy.

Finally, she had her happily ever after.

"I have to go pick up Wanda at the airport in an hour," she reminded him even as she tightened her arms around his shoulders and pulled him closer.

After a couple of visits to Seattle, her best friend had decided to leave Harrisons', accept Darius's job offer and move to the west coast. These days Rowyn couldn't stop smiling. And she owed it all to this man who had swept into her life and made her a princess in her personal fairy tale.

Her smile widened. Her father had been the first man to call her a princess and had engraved the words on her necklace. Last month, Darius had become the second when he'd added *mia principessa*—my princess—underneath the Korean endearment. If she hadn't been in love with him already, she would have fallen that day.

"I love you, Darius."

He lifted his head and stared down at her, the corner of his mouth lifted in a sexy quirk.

"I love you more, Mrs. Fiore."

READ ON FOR AN EXCERPT FROM
NAIMA SIMONE'S

SWEET SURRENDER

About Sweet Surrender

Killing the messenger is frowned upon. Okay, then... What about lying the messenger on the nearest flat surface and making her scream with pleasure?

From the moment Hayden Reynolds approaches Griffin Sutherland in the local, Florida dive bar, all he can think about is fisting her dark curls and stroking those gorgeous curves. But hell would freeze over before she allowed him to touch her because she's the woman he left behind five years earlier. And now she's there to deliver a message—an ultimatum—from his estranged father. Blackmail forces Griffin, black sheep of his powerful Texas family, back home to play nice. But the terms of his bargain say nothing about not satisfying his need for the woman he's never forgotten...never stopped wanting...

Hayden is no longer the naive girl who once fiercely loved a golden Sutherland and believed he and a maid's daughter could live happily ever after. Griffin broke her all those years ago, but she forced herself to pick up the pieces and move on. Now he's back in Texas, acting the part of the proper, dutiful son. But there's nothing *proper* about the detailed--dirty--descriptions of how he wants to touch her...take her... Though her body heats every time he's near, she refuses to surrender to his special brand of passion. Because Griffin may have returned home, but he's leaving again. But this time he won't take her heart with him...

Excerpt

A naked blonde walks into a bar with a poodle under one arm and a two-foot salami under the other...

Hayden frowned. What the hell was the rest of that joke?

She lifted the mug of tepid, dark brown beer, sniffed its yeasty scent, and lowered the glass to the scarred table with no small amount of disgust.

Hell, it didn't matter. The joke was funny in *Breakfast Club* when Judd Nelson was crawling through an air vent during Saturday detention. Not so much when she sat in a Florida dive bar that looked like something straight off the set of a biker B-movie. With said bikers eyeing her as if she were either a narc or serving up the same thing as the skinny blonde with the dark roots, double-D cups and denim skirt up to her See You Next Tuesday. And from the frequent trips to the dingy hallway that led to the restrooms, the woman either had a bladder the size of a pea, or she was serving up pussy like Waffle House hash browns.

And the heat. *God.* She tugged on the collar of her T-shirt, praying for even tiniest bit of circulation to cool her damp skin.

She lived in Texas so she was accustomed to hot-as-hell, but damn, Florida, with its smothering, almost tropical humidity, was a whole different animal. And with her curls starting to tighten into a big ass mane, she probably resembled one of those animals. Son-of-a-bitch, she'd only been in the Sunshine State for four hours, and she already hated it. If not for the work assignment that had sent her to this little backwater town and bar, she and her afro would be getting the hell outta Dodge.

Or Blackpool, Florida.

Why anyone with brains, ambition, or a need for a damn Big Mac would voluntarily settle in this wrong turn off I-10 stumped the hell out of her. Seriously. Not. One. McDonald's. From the looks of the clientele in this shit hole of a bar they obviously didn't give a damn about a healthy lifestyle. So that meant the town was just as she'd called it when she'd almost driven right past it: Fucked.

And didn't that just sum up the plethora of reasons why she was sitting in this godforsaken bar in this godforsaken town?

She'd earned a Bachelor's in Managerial Studies and an M.B.A. in Finance. At twenty-six years old, she was the personal assistant to one of the most powerful businessmen in the state of Texas—hell, the whole country. Yet, she'd been reduced to a pseudo-bounty hunter for his wayward son.

Not just any son, though.

Griffin Sutherland.

Her first lover. The man she'd once loved with all the passion of a too-stupid-to-live girl. The man who'd broken her heart and walked out on her without a backward glance or a word in five years.

Yep. Fucked.

But that was a lifetime—and an emotional lobotomy—ago.

She wasn't the same gullible, stars-in-her-eyes young girl Griffin had left sobbing in a fetal position on sheets still carrying the scent of Freshly Fucked. A year after stumbling around like a slightly-cleaner-not-as-bloody zombie, she'd gotten her ass in gear. He'd broken her, but out of the pain, she'd forged someone stronger, smarter, and driven. Someone who didn't take anyone's shit. Someone who wouldn't ever be cock-fodder for another man again.

Any love she'd harbored for Griffin Sutherland had been successfully torched and incinerated years ago by his indifference and silence. But, Joshua Sutherland wasn't privy to the history between her and his youngest son. As far as he knew, they'd been chummy during childhood and up until Griffin had abandoned his family five years ago. In his opinion, who better to send on this retrieval trip than a person his son actually liked?

She snorted.

Joshua would've been better off coming himself. Since "the help" hadn't been invited to Audrey Sutherland's—Joshua's wife and Griffin's mother—birthday party several months ago, Hayden hadn't seen Griffin when he'd returned to Houston to attend. Which was a blessing because ripping off his son's balls the first time she laid eyes on him in five years would've *probably* been just cause for being fired.

Still...she had to suck up her castrating urges. She hadn't failed a task given to her yet by Joshua, and dragging his black sheep son back to the family fold wouldn't be the first. Even if this was literally the last place she would rather be. And that included hell and Disney World on the 4th of July.

Sighing, she glanced up, searching for the waitress. Her beer was starting to not just look like piss but smell like it. Just as she caught the young woman's eye, a big hulk of a man with a black beard that had to break a record for bushiness, a leather vest and a chest full of tattoos winked at her. A shiver of *eew* skittered over her skin. Even if she did go for the Blackbeard the pirate look, was that a fucking swastika inked on the side of his neck? Apparently, being a member of the master race didn't prevent him from wanting to bone a Latina. Fucker.

A burst of raucous laughter yanked her attention from Blackbeard and almost drowned out the incongruous tinkle of the bell above the bar's entrance. She glanced up as three men stumbled through the doorway, shoving each other and tossing insults back and forth. She scanned their scruffy faces, stained T-shirts and jeans, hope craning its head up…only to drop back down in disgust. Nope. No Sutherland among them. The tip Joshua had received and passed on to her about this being Griffin's favorite watering hole must've been off.

Disgusted, she rose from her table. This was pointless. After four hours of waiting on him to show and being biker bait, she had to face the facts. Griffin probably wasn't showing up here tonight. That meant cruising the tiny town of Blackpool to find him. Oh fucking goody.

Muttering, she reached for her pocket and the cash she'd stashed there. She might have lived in a cottage on the estate of a million dollar mansion as a child and have resided in the Texas suburbs for the last few years, but Lorena Reynolds hadn't raised a fool. By carrying a purse into this pit, Hayden might as well loop a sign around her neck that declared "Beat the Shit Out of Me and Steal My Money" in red, bold, 48 point font.

"You boys enjoy. Drinks on me tonight."

She froze. That drawl. Slow, thick, and warm like the dark gold, heavy Karo syrup her mother used to pour over pan-fried cornbread when Hayden was younger. Delicious. Pure sin. And familiar. Too damn familiar.

Her ass dropped back to the stool as her heart kicked into a dull, ponderous thud in her chest. It'd been five years since she'd heard that voice. Since then it had teased her, whispered to her...seduced her.

"Open up for me, baby. That's it. Let me fuck that pretty mouth."
"This tight pussy is mine. Mine. Say it."
"I could fucking die in you, baby."

She blinked, beating back the memories that molasses-and-sex voice stirred, locking them away in the vault they'd somehow escaped from. Swallowing past the fist in her throat, she slowly rotated in the direction of the bar.

Wide shoulders and a broad chest tested the fortitude and determination of a plaid shirt stretched over a white T-shirt. Long, thick, muscular thighs encased in sturdy but worn denim. She could only catch a glimpse of his profile, but that small look revealed a man bigger, more muscled than the one in her memories. The formerly short blonde waves were now caught up in one of those pretty-boy man buns. Sure, this area of Florida could probably claim more than one Viking among its population, but only one man had ever incited the *oh shit* dip in her belly. Or that damn lick of heat in her veins.

Griffin.

The man had eviscerated her soul to the point that for a year after he left she hadn't wanted to do anything but lie in a bed and disappear under the covers. Yet, her body still recognized him as the only man who'd ever made it sing like fucking Pavarotti. She'd had one lover since him, and he'd failed in dragging a shattering, damn near mind-bending orgasm out of her like Griffin had. He hadn't made her crave his special brand of lust and passion that had her willing to do anything he asked.

Only Griffin had possessed that power.

God, how she hated him for it.

Hated herself for it.

But that was then. When she'd been a naïve girl eager to please the man on whom she'd believed the sun specifically rose and set. So what her pussy was like Pavlov's pitiful, trained dogs? She didn't want him, didn't need him. And last time she checked, her pussy followed her dictates, not the other way around.

Sliding from the chair once more, she straightened her shoulders, and strode toward the bar. The sooner she delivered her message to the bastard, the sooner she could call this mission accomplished and go home.

The headache-inducing blare of classic rock blaring from the ancient jukebox didn't soften, but damn if it didn't seem as if the volume lowered and every eye zeroed in on her as she cut a path through the tables and stools. Or maybe it was the pounding of her heart. She scoffed. That was ridiculous. What did she have to be afraid of? She'd faced down drunken good-ol'-boys who figured PA meant Piece of Ass. Confronting the man who'd ripped her heart out of her chest and used it for batting practice? Just another day on the job.

Wishing she had a baby wipe to clean the scarred surface of the barstool, she slid onto it.

"Hello, Griffin."

ALSO BY NAIMA SIMONE

Secrets and Sins Series
Gabriel
Malachim
Raphael
Chayot

Guarding Her Body Series
Witness to Passion
Killer Curves

Bachelor Auction Series
Beauty and the Bachelor
The Millionaire Makeover
The Bachelor's Promise
A Millionaire at Midnight

Lick Series
Only for a Night
Only for Your Touch
Only for You

Fairy Tales Unleased Series
Bargain with the Beast
A Perfect Fit

Other Titles
Flirting with Sin

ABOUT THE AUTHOR

USA Today Bestselling author Naima Simone's love of romance was first stirred by Johanna Lindsey, Sandra Brown and Linda Howard many years ago. Well not that many. She is only eighteen...ish. Though her first attempt at a romance novel starring Ralph Tresvant from New Edition never saw the light of day, her love of romance, reading and writing has endured. Published since 2009, she spends her days—and nights— writing sizzling romances with a touch of humor and snark.

She is wife to Superman, or his non-Kryptonian, less bullet proof equivalent, and mother to the most awesome kids ever. They all live in perfect, sometimes domestically-challenged bliss in the southern United States.

Connect with Naima through email (nsimonebooks@aol.com), through her website (www.naimasimone.com), on Twitter (https://twitter.com/Naima_Simone), on Facebook (https://www.facebook.com/naimasimoneauthor/), through her newsletter (http://naimasimone.com/contacts.html) or become a member of her fabulous Facebook Street Team (https://www.facebook.com/groups/376601019163211/).